INVASION: THE LOST CHAPTERS

A COMPANION WORK

DC ALDEN

There are thousands of books out there that dive deep into political sociology, religion and military strategy. *Invasion: Uprising* isn't one of them.

It's a military thriller set in an alternate future where the political and cultural landscape has shifted dramatically, an imagined stage on which this tale is set. Nothing more.

I hope you enjoy it.

DC Alden

You should know that **The Lost Chapters** is exactly that, a series of story lines and chapters that were cut from the original version of **Invasion** to make the book smaller and more marketable.

Those chapters went MIA for years before I found them on an old hard drive, so I decided to update them and add several new chapters to flesh out the **Invasion** world a little more.

The Lost Chapters doesn't run like a standard novel - more a series of short stories - but in any case, I do hope you enjoy it.

DC Alden

Listen not to the Unbelievers, but strive against them...

Quran, 25:52

DEAR RACHEL,

I hope you're well, and life across the ocean is everything you'd hoped for. Hard to believe a year has passed already, but for the record, I'm still missing you terribly. I won't labour that particular point. You know how I feel and always will.

Yes, I'm writing to you by hand. It feels quirky and odd, but somehow strangely liberating. The reason? I don't trust the internet anymore.

I can see you now, a satisfied smile spreading across that beautiful face, but the truth is you were right all along. So, I've made plans, but I'll get to that shortly.

I want to tell you about an interesting development. Last Friday evening the police came to the flat. They knocked on the door just before eight, two uniforms, both slovenly and overweight, and pretty aggressive into the bargain. In any case, they were there to investigate a complaint made about me. About a tweet in fact, but not one I'd posted; no, it was one I'd liked.

The tweet was written by a low-level political blogger,

1

criticising *Wazir* for his dubious military build-up and inflammatory anti-Western rhetoric. I don't remember doing it, but you know me, with my incessant scrolling and tapping. I asked the police if liking tweets was now an offence, and the scruffy little lesbian got quite flustered, warning me about promoting hate speech and the possibility of future arrest. I pushed back, asked them why it was 'hate speech' to criticise a despotic foreign national and his made-up Caliphate. The answer?

Blasphemy.

Yes, as unbelievable as it sounds, that's what she told me. I asked her how that works in British law and, of course, she didn't have an answer. I doubt either of them could spell the word. I asked them who'd made the complaint but they wouldn't divulge that information either. Quite frankly it was more like an interrogation than an investigation. And they seemed to know a lot about me too, where I worked, my friends, associates, previous comments I'd made on social media, that sort of thing. In any case, they told me that the anonymous complaint would be 'held on file' indefinitely, and they left me with several not-so-veiled threats ringing in my ears. So, that's it, my card is finally marked. I think you'd be quite proud of me.

Still, I was left with a feeling of general unease. I spent most of that evening thinking (glass of wine in hand, naturally). I thought about the encounter, the way the uniformed woman had blurted it out, and I wondered how blasphemy had entered the lexicon of police language. Maybe not 'how', but 'when'. And I thought about something you'd once said, about the police and judiciary being infiltrated, usurped, quietly enforcing a hidden agenda against the will of the people. Enforcing Sharia, in my case.

I sat in silence for much of that night, in my chair by the

window, watching the empty streets. It used to be so vibrant around here, especially on a Friday, but much has changed since you left us. A man was beaten to death on the high street last month, right outside that charity shop you used to enjoy pottering around. The victim was a city trader, and by all accounts very pissed. The locals, well, they frown on public drunkenness these days, especially in a 'religiously-sensitive area' as the police spokesperson called our little neck of the woods, and so the trader's subsequent beating barely made the news. The poor lad's life support was switched off a week later, and the investigation appears to have run its course, with not a single arrest to show for it. It seems the police are now complicit in covering up certain crimes these days, or at the very least protecting the perpetrators, but as you would've pointed out, they have form for these events: Rotherham, Rochdale, Oxford, Newcastle, ad infinitum.

I thought about us too. Remember all those parties and get-togethers, where I'd beg you not to mention politics? And when some poor, unsuspecting fool brought it up, you'd dive right in and dismantle their arguments and lofty opinions with your superior intellect and hugely impressive command of the facts. Lambs to the slaughter! But that never stopped me cringing and apologising on your behalf, did it? We'd leave early of course, and always in a huff, and later we'd fight. The invites dwindled, and soon we became persona non-grata, social outcasts. Destroyers of dinner parties. I should've stood by you then, but like everyone else, I was a coward. I didn't want to hear about Muslim expansion, Islamification, open borders, any of it. I just wanted us to be together. To live a normal life, as a normal couple. I was naive, I realise that now. It was only after we broke up that I became aware of the world around me. I'd become too *wrapped up in my own thoughts and feelings you see, too heavily invested in our relationship. As you well know, I wallowed in self-pity for a long time afterwards.*

Then one day the fog lifted.

I was on my way to work, waiting to cross the road, when I saw the advert on the side of a passing bus. It was a video of Wazir, ranting silently, eyes blazing, wagging his index finger at the sky in a continuous digital loop. The text beneath the video was in Arabic, wrapped around the bus like a neon garland, and I found out later that it was a Wazir speech about Western moral corruption or some such nonsense. On the side of a London bus, no less. I watched it crawl down the road, a rolling commercial for a man whose rise to power has been drenched in blood. Yet people walked on by, oblivious. There was no outcry, no political condemnation, just a silent, cowardly acceptance of the man and his message. I contacted the Advertising Standards Authority and complained. They told me to send an email, so I did. I never heard from them, but I'm pretty sure someone, somewhere, would've made a note of that.

So, I began to look at the world around me. I mean really look, like you'd urged me to do so many times. And what I saw troubled me. I saw a different city to the one our grandparents grew up in. I'm not saying it was all so much better back then, but, well, I think you know what I mean. I don't recognise my own neighbourhood anymore. The shops, the people, the minarets rising above the rooftops, it doesn't feel welcoming; were it not for the weather I could've been anywhere in Wazir's new Caliphate. I often feel like a trespasser, a stranger in a strange land, treated with disdain and total indifference. If I close my eyes, I no longer hear my own language. Part of me feels uncomfortable saying these things, yet I can't help but think that we've ceased moving forward, together, as a community, as a city. We're more divided now than ever, that's my gut feeling, and that division is being exploited, not least by Wazir himself.

They march in his support every weekend now, in their tens of thousands, right across the country. London, Birmingham, Manchester, and dozens of others towns and cities. The crowds are hostile, and certain flags are burned, while others belonging to terror groups and banned organisations are brandished with pride and impunity. Sky News, the BBC, they maintain a cowed silence, as they always have, despite these blatant provocations. And the media whores, well, they scramble to champion the right to free speech at every opportunity. But watch out if you have an opposing opinion. Or 'like' a tweet.

My eyes have been opened, Rachel. I can see the cracks you always spoke of, and it won't be long before they become fissures. A tectonic event must surely follow.

I've always thought that my future was relatively assured, that I'd go to work, pay my bills, that things would go on as they always have. But lately, I've been hearing things, in coffee shops, at work, on the street, like walking through a busy pub, catching snatches of conversation as one moves through the crowd. Whispered words, furtive looks. A contagion of fear, seeping through the city.

Remember that awful day when your father died? Remember when the call came, and I knew before you'd answered it, that somehow it was bad news? That's what I'm feeling now, Rachel. A sense of apprehension, of something building on the horizon. Sounds crazy, I know, but I can't shake it off. And I'm not the only one.

I attended a conference in Brussels last month, and someone there mentioned it too, a throwaway comment in the hotel bar about Muslim communities across Belgium suddenly withdrawing into themselves, suspicious of outsiders, watchful. A Dutch delegate said much the same thing. I tried to research the phenomenon on my return but suddenly the Internet isn't reliable anymore. It keeps dropping right across Europe, and no one knows why. And when it is working, well, social media is awash with pro-Wazir propaganda, much of it re-posted by our own politicians, media personalities and various other sycophants. Everyone is so desperate to appease, it's really quite sickening, but it's also feeding into my mounting...what, exactly? Dread, I suppose, though that seems overly dramatic. But the truth is, I'm frightened.

I said earlier I'd made plans. I'm serving notice at work and the flat is finally under offer. The economy is bad, I know that, and Beecham, well he's a decent enough Prime Minister, but I think things are only going to get worse. I won't get much for the place (I wish I'd sold up when you did) but it'll be enough to make a start elsewhere. America, in fact.

And no, I'm not stalking you. God forbid you would think that of me, but I've deliberated long and hard and come to the conclusion that it's the right choice. I considered Australia initially, but they seem hell-bent on importing their own problems, and besides, you know I don't care much for the heat. I thought about New Zealand too, but it just feels a little too remote. Who knows, maybe that'll be a good thing in the future, but right now it's not an option for me. So, I've decided on America. The land of the free, home of the brave. We Brits find all that jingoism a little amusing sometimes, but when Americans talk about defending freedom and democracy, they actually mean it. Not like us Europeans. Nowadays we cower and fawn in the face of aggression.

So, thankfully, my visa has been approved and I've managed to get a decent job with a big pharmaceutical in Denver. You know I love my outdoor pursuits, so I'm pretty sure I'll be happy there. And it's only a few hours from New York, so if you ever get the urge to visit, there'll always be a warm welcome waiting. It would be wonderful to see you again.

I will miss this green and pleasant land of course. And London, naturally. Spend enough time here and the city gets into the blood. The smells, the sounds, the people, the architecture, the vibrancy and the sheer bloody history, all built upon the backs of our ancestors. It's always felt like home. It's always energised me, made me feel truly alive and connected. And it's where I met you, which is why this ancient capital will always occupy a special place in my heart.

But it doesn't feel like home, not anymore. Something's changed, something fundamental and deeply troubling. I feel like I'm living in ancient Rome, the empire on the brink of collapse, and outside the gates, the Barbarians, slowly encircling the walls, watching, waiting, quietly preparing to invade. And what of us, who stand in their way? Our common identity has been eroded, our history and culture the subject of scorn and ridicule, our flag no better than the hated swastika. We are left with nothing to believe in, nothing to fight for. And ultimately, nothing worth defending.

Or maybe I'm being overly dramatic again. Time will tell no doubt, but I fear the worst.

I'll be leaving for Denver at the beginning of May, with a start date in June, which will give me time to settle in. I'll send you my contact details (by email this time - my arm is *actually aching!) so if you decide to drop me a line, well, it would make my year.*

I'm sorry how things turned out, Rachel. I turned my back on you when you needed me, and I shall live with that regret until my dying day. Yet in some strange way, our parting was a blessing for us both. You've made a new and better life for yourself, and my eyes were finally opened. I began to see what you've always seen, the rapidly changing face of Europe, the shifting sands beneath our feet, and carried on the wind, the distant drumbeat of war. And for that sudden awakening, I have only you to thank.

Now my instincts are telling me to run, while I still can. For the sakes of those I'm leaving behind, I pray that those instincts are wrong.

Love always,
Charlie x
10th February, 2029

Abdul Jalaf drove his Ford van up to the security gate, powered down the window, then offered his ID to the guard. After a cursory inspection, the barrier was raised and Abdul was waved through into the complex.

Creswell Armaments PLC had occupied the sprawling, well-guarded site just outside the town of Deepcut for fifty-three years. For the last eighteen months – and after passing what the facilities company laughingly referred to as a vetting procedure – Abdul had worked here for ten hours a day, six days a week, repairing broken windows, fixing door locks, changing light bulbs and working on a multitude of other tasks that were required of him as a maintenance contractor.

He was a familiar face around the site, always cheerful, polite, helpful. To his colleagues, he was friendly but quiet, never indulging in the gossip and banter that often helped to relieve the low-paid drudgery of their employment. Abdul was punctual, hardworking, and always willing to cover for others when sickness or absenteeism struck.

After ten months at Creswell, Abdul made supervisor,

9

giving him access to the more sensitive parts of the factory. He moved around restricted areas freely, ensuring health and safety compliance, hygiene standards and the carrying out of essential maintenance works. He became part of the landscape, his movements never questioned, his presence in restricted areas acknowledged and ignored. And that suited the facility supervisor perfectly.

Because Abdul Jalaf was a ghost.

Although his heart beat regularly and his brain functioned as it should, inside Abdul was dead to the world around him. His reason for living died the day an Israeli F-16 fighter dropped a smart bomb on the home of a Hamas leader in Ramallah, just as his wife was passing on the street outside with their twin six-year-old girls. Abdul remembered hearing the detonation, feeling the shockwave through his feet, his immediate reaction one of sudden dread as he dropped the crate of vegetables he was carrying and rushed to the scene.

He'd arrived just as the broken bodies of his girls were being lifted from the rubble. The pain he'd felt at that moment, as his brain fought to process the gaping wounds, the dust and blood, was indescribable. Laid out on the rubble-strewn street, along with his dead wife, Abdul had caressed their small, shattered corpses, begging Allah to breathe life back into them, cursing Him when his prayers went unanswered, screaming as his hands were prised from theirs. He wailed, lashing out at those around him as his family's bodies, along with a dozen others, were loaded into ambulances and ferried to the local morgue. It was a trip possessed of its own finality, Abdul knew. The dead were to be mourned, then buried quickly in the West Bank. He would've lain with them in that butcher's shop if they'd let him. Instead, he was taken to a relative's home, sedated, and left to grieve.

Pain consumed him. He couldn't eat or sleep, refused to talk to those who tried to help him. He went back to his empty home and cried in the darkness. The weeks turned to months. Time healed nothing.

And then one day, Yussef Al-Mahji arrived at the house.

It was a warm summer evening. Abdul was sitting on his porch sipping a cup of bitter coffee when he saw the dark Mercedes bouncing along the track towards his smallholding, watched the powerful saloon brake to a halt in a cloud of dust, and scrambled to his feet when Al-Mahji climbed out of the rear of the vehicle, briefcase in hand.

Yussef Al-Mahji was a well-known figure in Ramallah, a businessman both respected and feared. The families of those who had been shot, bombed or had died in Israeli custody were virtually guaranteed a visit by Al-Mahji. There would be words of comfort, and often some American dollars, all gratitude for their sacrifice. But there was nothing for the civilians, no death dividend for the victims of collateral damage. So, what did he want?

Abdul shook the offered hand as Al-Mahji stepped onto his porch.

"Greetings, brother," said Al-Mahji.

Abdul nodded. Despite his visitor's reputation, he was unafraid. There was nothing Al-Mahji could do to him that could possibly cause him any more pain than the loss of his family. Yet, he was intrigued.

"Would you like coffee? The pot is still warm."

"Thank you. It has been a long day."

Abdul poured a fresh cup, and for a while they sat in silence, watching the chickens scratch around in the dust.

Then Al-Mahji turned and said, "The stillness of this place must be a terrible burden to bear."

Abdul looked at his guest. The man *knew*. "Sometimes I can still hear the girls laughing, my wife cooking in the kitchen. Their ghosts haunt me."

"An unimaginable blow," Al-Mahji agreed, "especially for a man such as yourself. An innocent farmer, a man who toils the land, feeds his community. A man whose only wish was to provide for his family. Live a quiet life."

Abdul said nothing as Al-Mahji picked up the briefcase at his feet and laid it on the table. He snapped open the locks and lifted the lid.

"I have something to show you, Abdul. It was found in the rubble on the day of the Jew attack." Al-Mahji reached inside the briefcase and handed over a sheet of twisted metal the size of a paperback book.

Abdul took it, turned it over in his hands. It was dark green in colour, with black stencilled letters and some scorch marks around the —

He dropped the fragment on the table as if it were red hot. He stood up, knocking his chair over.

"No," he whispered.

Al-Mahji placed the fragment back inside the briefcase and snapped it shut. "A Paveway Two guided missile. A smart weapon, as the Infidels like to call them. What is smart about killing women and children, eh?"

"Why did you bring this, this thing here, to my house?" demanded Abdul.

Al-Mahji waved him back into his seat. "This *thing* is part of the missile actuation system. We know where it was made and by whom."

"We? You mean Hamas, no?"

"Hamas is only a tiny cog in the machine. But that is not

why I am here, Abdul. Islam has many enemies. We are at war and have been throughout history, this you know. But our victories have always been small. Rarely do we achieve a major coup, one in which the world will sit up and take notice."

Abdul frowned. "But New York, the twin towers?"

"A magnificent operation, but not by our hand. The Godless killed their own to justify their unholy war on Islam. Look what has happened since that day. Millions of Muslims have been butchered in Iraq and Afghanistan, their homelands desecrated by the Unbelievers. Then there is the question of the oil. The West takes what it wants, grows fat on what God has bestowed on our people by birth. They will be stopped, of course. Already they have begun to fear the rise of Wazir, the erasing of borders drawn by the West. The Caliphate grows in size and power every day. A reckoning is coming, Abdul Jalaf. You can be a part of that, should you wish it."

Al-Mahji fished a pack of cigarettes from his pocket and lit one, leaning back in his chair.

Allowing his words to sink in, Abdul knew. He may be a simple farmer but he was not stupid. He knew why Al-Mahji had come. And he was ready.

"Whatever it is you want of me, I will do it."

Abdul leaned on the table, blew smoke from the side of his mouth. "You worked in England some years ago, yes? Before your father died and left you this place? Your English is good?"

Abdul nodded. "I still listen to the BBC."

"Good. Then this is what you will do. First, you will be trained to fight. Then, when you are ready, you will travel to England, as a refugee. You will gain employment at the factory where the missile parts were made. This will be arranged for you. You will then perform your duties quietly and diligently until some time in the future. That is when you will go to work with the bomb and the bullet. The day you will kill those who have destroyed not just your family but also many others. You will die of course, but you will have avenged the innocent. Then you will join your loved ones in Paradise. This is what I am asking you to do." Al-Mahji pushed back his chair and stood. "You have a few minutes to decide."

Abdul watched him step off the porch and wander back to the Mercedes. The driver got out, and they stood chatting quietly. *So, it has come to this.* It was as if Al-Mahji knew about his sleepless nights, the dreams of bloody revenge visited on his family's killers. His life was empty, his home a living tomb, haunted by visions of a life now passed. He missed his girls so much. The years stretched out before him, bleak, empty. This wasn't living, it was waiting for death, longing for a time when he would see his wife and children again. In Paradise.

Al-Mahji turned as Abdul walked towards the Mercedes.

"You will get me in there? Into the lair of the beast?"

"Europe's doors are wide open. It will not be a problem," Al-Mahji assured him.

Abdul nodded. "So be it."

He very nearly smiled at the memory.

There had been many times since – during his training at the desert camps, his journey west posing as a persecuted migrant, his first few weeks in an overcrowded immigration centre, the bed and breakfast in Lewisham – that his resolve had wavered and he'd wept silently under the thin blanket for a dead family, the soil of his homeland underfoot and the warm sun on his face. But there was no turning back. He'd prayed hard for strength and Allah had finally answered him.

He'd been offered the job at Creswell as promised, had settled into the local community, living his life in this damp, grey country for almost three years. Far to the east, the Caliphate had risen, and Wazir had come to power. Western governments were cautious, yet the hand of diplomatic friendship and international cooperation was offered and taken by the Infidels. As time passed, Abdul's hopes of striking his enemy had begun to fade.

Almost. And then one day, just as Al-Mahji had promised, the signal had come, the text message he'd waited for so long. Abdul's spirits soared. He felt truly elated, eager to fulfil his destiny. All he needed now was the final *go* signal. That, too, would soon come.

After passing through the security gate he parked his car outside the maintenance block and wheeled his portable tool cart into the building. He locked the door to his tiny office. It was time to prepare.

He went to his personal locker, a grey, battered metal cabinet that stood against the wall. He pulled out the overalls, the cleaning rags, boxes of bleach and scrubs. Hidden beneath it all was a heavy steel toolbox. Abdul removed the padlock, opened it, then took out the parts wrapped in thick plastic that he'd carefully smuggled in over several weeks. With skill and dexterity, he quickly assembled the AK-12 assault rifle. He racked the cocking handle, checked the action, hefted the weight in his hands. The AK-12 was a magnificent weapon, a weapon he had come to respect and admire during his training in the desert, and one that felt familiar to him once more. He reached into his portable toolbox and retrieved the six fully-loaded magazines hidden under his other tools. Finally, he slipped a padlock through the hasp and locked it.

He checked his watch; nearly three o'clock.

He would make his rounds shortly, ensuring that his access pass would function correctly, allowing him access to the restricted areas for the last time.

He smiled: in a few short hours he would be finally able to avenge the death of his beautiful wife and his two little princesses.

And those Infidel scientists, those doers of Satan's work, would know the meaning of bloody retribution.

THE SPOTTER, IBRAHIM, TRACKED THE MINIVAN through powerful binoculars as the ministerial convoy slowed, then passed through the distant school gates. Two of the police motorcycle outriders parked their bikes across the entrance while the other two followed the three-vehicle convoy up towards the main building and the waiting crowd.

Ibrahim was two hundred metres away, observing proceedings through the grimy, mesh-covered window of a roadside portacabin. Behind him, the interior was like any other construction company shack; a collection of battered metal chairs and tables, strewn with discarded newspapers and filthy coffee mugs, a small kitchenette, a sink full of dirty plates. A news channel played quietly on the portable radio perched on top of a once-white refrigerator.

Ibrahim adjusted the focus ring as he continued his observations. A few minutes ago he'd briefed his team for the final time. Now they were outside by the road, wearing yellow jerkins and hardhats, performing their roles like the best of actors as they shovelled sand from one heap to another, and poured over fake plans. Yet unlike actors or construction workers, the tools that lay close to hand were those of soldiers; RPG 32's, H&K assault rifles, pistols, smoke and fragmentation grenades. Tools of war.

The deception was working well, Ibrahim noted. The construction company supervisor was a Believer, as was the council official who'd approved the works. No one had questioned the *Pavement Closed* signs, or the taped off and suspended bus stop. This was London, after all. These things were normal.

Ibrahim, keeping his distance from the window, tracked the convoy as brake lights flared and it slowed to a stop outside the main school building. He checked his watch – two more hours before they would strike – and ran over the schedule in his head once more. The Prime Minister would arrive at the Greenwich Academy at two forty-five, deliver his speech to assorted governors, teachers and pupils, then leave the building at five pm precisely. The intelligence also told him that the convoy would approach the school by one route, then leave by another, passing the construction site directly outside. It was at that point, when one of Ibrahim's men would drive the waiting truck into the first security vehicle, that the trap would be sprung. Everyone was to die, except for the Prime Minister. His vehicle would be disabled, the man himself captured. Ibrahim was confident the plan would work.

His team were experienced fighters, from Aleppo, Gaza and Mosul, all veterans in the art of ambush and street fighting. Over the previous three days, they'd choreographed the snatch in a disused factory in the Midlands. They had the schedule, the routes, the weapons and the motivation. All they needed now was the target. Once in their custody, Prime Minister Beecham was to be taken to a safe house, a remote farm in Kent, and detained there until the airborne troops descended from the sky and London was secured. That hour was drawing near, and Ibrahim found it difficult to contain his excitement.

He watched with interest as the lead and rear vehicles disgorged their security teams and the welcome party grinned and clapped like clockwork monkeys. The door to the Prime Minister's minivan slid open. First out were his close protection officers, scanning the excited faces of children and parents in the crowd, the panting, salivating dignitaries. They were efficient yet relaxed, their pistols kept firmly out of sight. No one was expecting any trouble.

He switched focus to the welcome party, a mix of young and old, pressing forward with idiotic grins on their faces, their camera phones held high. A ripple of flashes announced the PM's appearance from inside the vehicle. Ibrahim gripped the binoculars, his heart beating a little faster now; this was to be his first ever sighting of Beecham, and he was eager to see his prey in the flesh.

The legs that swung out onto the pavement were smooth and shapely. A woman stood, her hand extended, and she greeted the waiting dignitaries. Ibrahim's eye lingered on the tanned limbs a little too long, and he felt a momentary flash of guilt. The whore had distracted him, the devil tempting him from his holy mission. His first bullet would be for her.

He swivelled back to the minivan and waited for Beecham's appearance. And waited. No one else appeared, and then the whore leapt into his vision again. She was smiling and shaking hands, working the crowd. The Infidels were all smiling too, holding out their paws to be gripped and pumped like the udders of a cow —

Then it hit him.

The Prime Minister wasn't there.

The whore, it was Beecham's wife. For reasons unknown, she had taken his place. Ibrahim watched for several more minutes until the party had moved inside and the crowd had dispersed, until the convoy had disappeared around the side of the building. He lowered the binoculars and laid them on the table. He sat down, ran his hands over his face. His was a mission of huge importance, the honour of his selection the greatest of his life. And now this. The disappointment he felt was crushing, like a physical weight on his shoulders. There was anger too, a sudden rush of fury that would only be satisfied by leading his team down to the school right now and killing everyone in sight. But that would be foolish, dangerously so. No, there were procedures in place, contingency plans to fall back on. Communication was key. That had to be his priority now.

He took a calming breath and thumbed open his phone, dialled the memorised number, delivered the abort code phrase. He went to the door, beckoned his team back inside the portacabin, ordered them to recover their weapons and head back to the safe house in Catford. He saw their faces, felt the pain of their disappointment, but they would soon recover. Fresh orders would not be long in coming.

And they could be assured that there would be plenty of other targets that evening.

THE ENCRYPTED ABORT MESSAGE WAS RELAYED ACROSS Europe to a sand-blown military airstrip in Libya. There it was deciphered and printed, then handed to a waiting messenger.

The messenger swallowed hard when he was told the recipient's name. He hurried outside into the hot afternoon sun, snapped on his goggles and crunched the vehicle into gear. The drive was a relatively short one, less than a kilometre, out towards the runway apron and the loading area. To get there he had to take the access road, the one that ran parallel to the taxiway that was now crammed with the biggest collection of military transport craft the corporal had ever seen in his life, their turboprop engines creating a dust storm that billowed across the desert floor and almost blotted out the sun.

He stamped on the brakes and brought the Humvee to a halt next to an Airbus A400 military transport aircraft and watched as two columns of heavily laden paratroopers shuffled up its rear loading ramp. It was just one aircraft in a long line of planes that stretched the length of the two-kilometre runway, and each one was in the process of loading men and equipment. The noise was deafening as scores of already-loaded planes rumbled past, taxiing for take off. That dust cloud could probably be seen for miles, the corporal thought.

He climbed out of his jeep and approached a small knot of senior officers conferring beneath the wing of the giant transport. Just beyond the aircraft, yet another plane thundered down the runway and lifted off into a clear blue sky. The messenger watched it claw its way upwards, to join the other planes that had already taken off and were now circling several thousand feet above.

"Yes, what is it?"

The messenger stepped forward quickly, flipped up his goggles and saluted, his knees suddenly weak. So this was him. The general above all others, the man who had the ear of the Holy One. General Faris Mousa. He handed over the message slip. The general snatched it, scanned it, then dismissed the messenger with a flick of his hand.

The messenger blew his cheeks out in relief. It wasn't a good idea for a lowly corporal such as himself to get too close to these men of power. You never knew what mood they were in, and if you somehow incurred their wrath, well, that would be too bad. The penal battalions were full of men who'd crossed an officer's path.

He jumped back into his jeep and drove off, back past the unending line of aircraft. Whatever was in that message was bad news, because after reading it, General Mousa had cursed angrily and torn the message slip to shreds.

Abdul wheeled his tool cart into the high-security weapons research block and smiled. Behind the desk, Gareth the security guard looked up, smiled back, then buzzed him through the glass doors.

Abdul swiped through another set of security doors and then he was inside the belly of the beast, the research corridor, the glass wall to his left stretching away to the end of the block. Behind that wall, engineers in lab coats and plastic eyewear beavered away at their computers and workbenches. One of the engineers, an overweight blonde woman, looked up and smiled as he rolled his cart past. Abdul nodded politely, offered a wave. He had seen the whore many times, mostly in the lab but more often late at night, outside the company social club, drunk with alcohol, pressing herself up against a man and not always the same one. He would enjoy killing her.

He strolled to the end of the corridor and stopped outside a storeroom. He bumped the door open with his cart and wheeled it inside, closing the door behind him. Moving quickly now, he lifted the AK-12 out of the tool box and set it on the shelf. Then he wriggled out of his company over-alls, revealing the tactical chest rig he'd slipped on earlier. He checked the fully-loaded magazines, that the rounds were seated correctly, then placed them in the front pouches of the rig. He spent a minute or so ensuring that they could be easily retrieved and swiftly loaded, then gave the AK-12 a final once over. He slung it over his head, loaded a mag, cocked the weapon, then flicked the selector to semi-auto.

He was ready.

Abdul let the weapon hang across his chest as he closed his eyes and offered up his hands to God. He prayed for a keen eye and a steady hand, but most of all he prayed for time, that he would have enough to finish His work. Satisfied that his prayers had been heard, Abdul reached for the door handle and stepped out into the corridor.

It was an odd sensation, to be standing in his place of employment, now armed with an automatic rifle instead of a mop or a broom. Beyond the glass wall, the *Kuffar* continued Satan's work, unaware of the Angel of Death standing only metres away, watching them. For the first time in many years, Abdul felt free, liberated from the cloak of timid conformity and domestic servitude he'd been forced to endure during his employment at Creswell Armaments.

And still, no one noticed him.

Beyond the glass the Infidels wandered to and fro, oblivious to his presence. Abdul glanced up at the black eye of the CCTV camera along the corridor. It was only a matter of seconds before someone spotted him. Before someone tried to stop him from carrying out God's work. He jammed the rifle into his shoulder.

It was time to begin.

He brought the muzzle of the weapon up and squeezed the trigger. The AK roared, deafening. Glass shattered, and casings zinged across the corridor floor. His first target, a white-coated tech with a ponytail took two rounds in the back and dropped to the floor. Abdul switched aim, shooting the frozen ones who stared at him with wide, uncomprehending eyes. Screams echoed throughout the building.

From the corner of his eye, he saw the security doors fly open and Gareth appeared, shouting into a radio. Abdul smiled, and Gareth froze, his tiny brain unable to process what he was seeing. *Abdul the maintenance man, killing everyone in sight.* Abdul was still smiling when he shot Gareth in the chest.

He turned his attention back to the main target, stepping over the shattered threshold and into the laboratory itself. Glass crunched under his shoes. People scattered in all directions, like cockroaches exposed to the light. Some ran for a door at the far end of the laboratory.

The fire escape. No!

Abdul ran after them. The door was still closed, the small corridor jammed with twenty or so *Kuffar* desperate to escape, screaming, clawing and pushing, terrified faces glancing over their shoulders. But there would be no escape, Abdul silently promised them. He flicked the AK's selector to full auto and emptied the remainder of the magazine into the tightly pressed bodies. Several fell like skittles. He ejected the magazine, let it clatter to the floor, and loaded a fresh one. The fire door crashed open, and daylight flooded the corridor. Abdul opened fire, hitting several more before the survivors piled outside, screaming.

Behind them, the wounded, dead and dying lay where

they fell. Some were crying and wailing, some trying to crawl their way out of the bloody heap. Abdul shot them all.

That's when he heard the woman behind him, her sobs for help. He spun around, marched back into the main lab. *The blonde whore.* She was stumbling across the floor towards him, her chubby arms cradling the slippery pink rope of her own entrails, her lab coat drenched in blood. Her face was a white mask of concentration, her eyes locked on his as she muttered his name, begging for help. Then her legs buckled and she fell to the floor. Abdul watched her as she tried to stand up, still clutching her stomach, her feet slipping on the blood-slicked floor like a new-born foal. She looked up at him, eyes pleading, all hope gone. Abdul answered her silent prayer and shot her in the face.

He heard something crash, saw a couple of cockroaches dart from their hiding place, desperate to escape. Abdul cut them down with a short burst. He worked his way around the room quickly, flushing them all out, killing them where they cowered, chopping them down as they ran. There was no mercy for anyone, and Abdul could feel the adrenaline rushing through his body, filling him with an exultation he'd never felt before. It was blood-lust, and he was intoxicated by the power of life and death it gave him over the vermin around him. But there would be no mercy for the Unbelievers. Only death.

He cleared a sudden stoppage, then realised everyone in the lab was dead, the floor soaked in the blood of his enemy. Abdul smiled. His place in Paradise was assured. Soon he would join his family, but until then he would go in search of more targets and send as many to hell as he could.

Alarms filled the laboratory, wailing and screeching. Red emergency lights washed across walls and ceilings.

Abdul made his way back to the fire escape, stomping over the carpet of dead bodies, and stepped outside.

Well-tended grass areas separated the single-storey buildings, but there was no one in sight. A hundred metres away to his left, the access road and the main administration buildings. As he watched, several figures broke cover and sprinted for the gate. Abdul tracked them through his battle sight and fired, stitching rounds into the first three runners. The others vaulted over the bodies and kept going. As his ears stopped ringing Abdul thought he heard something else, above the wail of multiple alarms.

He thought he heard gunshots.

He spun around as a man and a woman charged around the corner towards him, hand in hand. Abdul recognised them both, the Human Resources director and his young secretary. Abdul slung his rifle behind his back and called out to them.

"This way, Mister Hall! Quickly!"

They veered towards him. The director slowed and the secretary dropped to her knees on the grass. Two large black smears of mascara streaked her face as she sobbed hysterically. The director's face was ashen.

"There's shooting at the main gate!" he blurted. "What the bloody hell is going on?"

"They're dead, all of them," sobbed his secretary.

At that moment Abdul felt the connection, and joy filled his heart. There were others out there, just like him, Soldiers of Allah, fighting close by. He was no longer alone. He would find them, join forces, die alongside his Brothers and Sisters. But he had to move fast. He swung the AK from behind his back.

"Oh my God!" screamed the girl. Abdul shot her in the

head, skull and brain matter spraying across the grass. The director raised his hands.

"Please, I'm begging you, I have a family."

"As did I," Abdul growled. He raised the barrel, jammed it into the man's right eye and pulled the trigger.

He stepped over the body and ran towards the access road. He paused at the end of the research building, yanked a black IS scarf from his pocket and wrapped it around his head. Now his Brothers and Sisters would recognise him as one of their own.

He peered around the side of the building. Dead bodies were scattered across the access road and the windows of the security building were peppered with bullet holes. Three police cars were slewed across Creswell's main entrance, their occupants armed and taking cover behind them, unaware of Abdul's appearance to their rear. They fired their weapons, aiming towards the MOD depot across the road. So, his people were there, on their own mission. He would make his move, link up with them. But first, he would kill the policemen.

He bent low, running across the open space towards the car park by the main gate. He burrowed into the maze of tightly parked cars, weaving his way closer to the perimeter fence. He crouched behind a BMW saloon and peered through the window. He hadn't been seen, but he didn't have a clear field of fire either. He needed to break cover, get closer to the Infidel police, take them out with one long burst.

He saw a shadow slide across the BMW's rear window, the silhouette of someone creeping up on him. He turned —

The flash blinded his eyes. The world tumbled upside down and his head hit something hard.

When his senses caught up with him he realised he was

lying on his back between the cars, looking up at the sky. A figure loomed over him, wearing a military uniform. He reached down, dragged the AK over Abdul's head, let his skull thump back onto the tarmac. The soldier's face was twisted with hate.

"I'll take that, cunt."

He saw the man's boot hover over his face and then it came down hard. Abdul felt bones break, and the sight in one eye left him. Then the Infidel was gone.

He felt no pain, only a numbness that enveloped his whole body. He was paralysed, and close to death, that much he knew.

The sound of gunfire faded. Through his good eye, he watched the summer sky above him, the most beautiful shade of blue he'd ever seen, and then he saw a bird, drifting high above him on the warm evening thermals. He thought he heard it cry, as if it were calling his name, but that wasn't possible, was it?

A shiver ran through his body and suddenly he found it difficult to breathe. His vision blurred and he couldn't see the bird anymore, couldn't hear its cry. Then the blue sky above him grew dark.

He heard his daughters' laughter somewhere, out there in the gathering darkness, and his heart sang. Then he saw her, his beloved wife, coming towards him out of the gloom. She was smiling, but suddenly her smile faded. Shadows swirled, enveloped her. The darkness loomed, impenetrable. Eternal.

There is no Paradise, was his final, fearful realisation.

Then Abdul Jalaf's world turned black.

It was the sudden rise in chatter outside his office that distracted Chief Inspector Chris Hunt from his emails.

He tutted, irritation spiking. Emails were important, vitally so if one wanted to rise through the ranks of the Metropolitan Police Service. Many of his colleagues moaned and groaned about their bulging inboxes, but not Chris. He knew the opportunities that lay therein, the call for volunteers for Pride events, the diversity symposiums, the outreach trips to the local mosque; all of these were unmissable opportunities for a career officer like Chris. They were chances to impress his superiors, to curry favour with community leaders, to ingratiate himself with the decision makers in HR. His inbox was a treasure trove of just such opportunities, and interruptions were unwelcome. A slammed door would send the right message to the operators outside.

He stood up and walked around his large, tidy desk. Through the half-open blind, he saw someone jog past the glass wall of his office. Chris peered through the slats, watched the guy drop into his chair, fix his headset in place. Chris frowned. The man looked rattled. He looked around the Special Operations Room, at the rows of operators hunched over their terminals; every one of them appeared to be engaged in some urgent business. He felt the sudden rise in tension as if the air itself was charged. He smoothed down his thinning hair and yanked open his office door.

A nearby operator sprang to her feet. She saw Chris approaching and said, "He's been shot."

Before he could formulate an answer Chris' eyes were drawn to the CCTV wall behind her, a high-tech chess-board of suddenly confusing images; people running across roads, panicked crowds, smoke, cars careering through traffic —

The room plunged into darkness.

Chris' heart began pounding in his chest.

A moment later emergency lights blinked, flickered on, bathing the control room in cold white light. People started calling out, status reports, demands for information. The CCTV feeds were dead, likewise the police radio and phone systems in the control room. Operators were punching keyboards, shouting into headsets. A voice boomed.

"Stay where you are, everyone. Main power should kick back in at any second."

Chris turned, saw Inspector Mark Meloy striding towards him. Meloy was ten years older, popular around the department, possessed of a natural authority and a lot of operational experience with a variety of front line units. Chris was quietly jealous of that experience but knew that ultimately, in an organisation like the Metropolitan Police, it was a political skill set that would win the day. Meloy was plod, pure and simple, his card already quietly marked.

Reaching Inspector would be the pinnacle of his career. He beckoned the man into his office.

"What the fuck's going on, guv? I was in the shitter when the lights went out."

"Not certain," Chris replied, cringing at Meloy's directness. He walked around his desk, saw his frozen laptop screen, tapped at the spacebar. Nothing.

Meloy snatched at his desk phone without permission, punched the keypad. "Dead," he muttered. "Intranet is down, radios too. And no one has a mobile signal. Not a drill then, unless you know different, guv?"

"Someone was shot," Chris said. His mind was racing. *Think! What should I do?*

Meloy was already marching outside. "Who's dealing with the shooting?" he bellowed across the SOR.

Chris followed him, approached the female operator with the raised hand. "You said someone was shot?"

"Yes, sir, an officer on foot patrol in Westminster. I lost him when the radio net dropped."

"We had a flood of emergency shouts," said another. "I saw at least one explosion on the monitors, outside Charing Cross station. Looks like a major terror attack, sir."

"We don't know anything, yet," Chris warned, his mouth suddenly dry.

"We know enough," Meloy snapped. He turned to the room. "Sit back down, get ready to start processing calls. We're going to be swamped as soon as that power kicks in, and the boys and girls out on the street are going to need us, got it?" There was a murmur of acknowledgement around the room. "Good. Keep the chatter down and stand by."

Chris folded his arms, fumed silently. "My office," he ordered Meloy. He hurried behind his desk and sat down, the symbol of his seniority now firmly between them.

"Right Mark, I think we should start documenting everything, get it all down while it's fresh in our minds, create a timeline of — "

"All due respect, sir, but that can wait. We need to focus on our comms. If the intranet and phones are out we'll need runners between the floors. We'll need pens, notepads, assign some of our operators to specific departments. We can configure the radios too, set them for local comms, walkie-talkie mode, until the network is back up. We'll need to secure this location too, get a couple of extra bodies on the door. And we need to check if the back-up site is offline too."

So *bloody practical,* Chris fumed. He hadn't thought of any of those solutions. No, his focus was making the *right* decisions, so blame, if any were to be attributed at some later point, would be directed elsewhere, laid at someone else's door. And he would document this conversation anyway, ensure that most of Meloy's suggestions became his own. That's how one advanced in the Metropolitan Police Service, Chris knew.

He flinched as a dull boom rumbled overhead. Outside in the SOR, light fittings swung lazily to and fro. A fine mist of dust drifted on the air.

"Bomb," Meloy growled, "a close one too." He poked his head outside the office. "Back in your seats," he barked, "and keep the chatter down. First-aiders?" Half a dozen hands went up in the air. "Grab every kit you can find, check the contents, make sure we're useful if called upon."

Chris simmered behind his desk. Meloy's decisiveness was making him feel increasingly impotent. He got to his feet. "Let's see what's happening upstairs."

"Negative. We need to be here, guv. When the power's back we're going to get battered.

"*If* the power comes back. It's been several minutes now. No phones, no radios, no computers. And what about the backup systems? It's designed to switch to battery power, no?"

"True enough," Meloy muttered, watching the room outside.

The ground shook again beneath their feet. Chris put his hand on the doorframe to steady himself. It felt like an earthquake, like the violent tremor that shook San Francisco a couple of years ago while Chris was holidaying there. He'd cowered like a child in the bathtub, and it had taken all of Anton's gentle coaxing just to get him to continue their vacation. Chris briefly wondered where his husband was now. Anton was a fashion designer, had a studio in Hackney, close to their flat in Islington. He'd be fine, Chris decided. Anton was sensible, would go home and wait. Chris wondered when he'd get home himself, in light of what was happening above them.

Another series of heavy detonations rippled through the room. Chris looked up at the ceiling. The SOR was four floors below ground level. Above that, twenty-three stories of glass, steel and concrete piled high above them. If that lot came down they'd all be buried alive. He felt the panic rising in his chest.

"We're going upstairs," Chris decided, pushing past Meloy and heading for the door.

"Your place is here, guv. I'll go, take a couple of the lads with me."

"I need to find out what's going on, connect with the leadership team," Chris snapped over his shoulder. He noticed he was leaving a trail of footprints in the dust behind him. He heard Meloy curse in his wake.

"Keep an eye on your systems," Meloy bellowed across the SOR. "We'll be back shortly."

Chris marched through the lifeless security doors and into the corridor outside. It was gloomy, the air thick with dust. Blue emergency lights barely lit the walls. Chris coughed violently. His sinuses were suffering already. He jammed a handkerchief against his nose and mouth and marched towards the elevators at the end of the corridor. He felt a hand on his arm, tugging.

"Wait, guv."

Chris spun around. "D'you mind?"

"If we're going topside we should grab our stabbies and belts, just in case."

Chris considered the suggestion, nodded. It was a good idea. When they made contact with management it would set a good impression.

In the shadows of the locker room, Chris took out his stab vest and wrapped it on. It had been a while since he'd worn it and it felt tight around his torso. *You're getting fat,* he chided himself. He clicked his utility belt around his waist, felt for the handle of his baton. It felt alien to him. He'd never used it in anger and hopefully would never have to.

Meloy loomed out of the shadows, looking every inch the frontline officer he'd been all his life. And had no doubt used his baton on many occasions, Chris assumed. Distasteful as the thought was, Chris felt quietly reassured by the lummox's presence.

"Okay, let's find out what's going on," he said as authoritatively as he could muster.

He led the way back out into the corridor and towards the darkened lobby. He could see the elevators were powerless but he stabbed the buttons anyway. Nothing.

"Stairs," Meloy pointed.

Chris followed obediently, decided to let Meloy have his lead, be the first to confront whatever it was they were about to confront. Just in case.

The door of the stairwell slammed behind them, and the two policemen found themselves in a dark, concrete stairwell. Dull blue emergency lights glowed on the upper landings, but the light faded every few seconds.

"Emergency batteries are losing power."

"Already?" Chris spluttered. He didn't want to be trapped in a near-black stairwell.

He ducked as a series of dull booms shook the walls. They were louder now, their violence rattling the rail beneath Chris' hand. He let go, pulled the torch from his belt, shone it upwards. The stairs switchbacked up into darkness.

"What the fuck is happening up there?" Meloy whispered.

"Maybe it's a gas main letting go?"

"No chance," Meloy snorted. "Those are bombs, and fucking big ones." He shone his own torch upwards, the beam of light playing over the concrete walls that disappeared into blackness. "We're looking at coordinated terror attacks, vehicle-borne IEDs, multiple shooters, who knows."

Meloy slapped him on the arm. "C'mon, let's go."

Chris found himself following his subordinate up the stairs, unable to process the situation, his boots scraping on the dusty concrete. By the time they reached the car park level, Chris was puffing hard. Meloy was barely out of breath, he noticed. Chris cursed again, Meloy proving himself to be the man of the hour, a natural leader. Everything that Chris wasn't. He took a moment to get his heart rate down, the blood rushing loudly in his head.

"Listen," Meloy whispered. "That's the civil defence siren."

Chris cocked his ear. Then he heard it, a mournful, fearful wail that must be deafening out on the streets. He swallowed hard. His fear was rising fast, clouding his judgement. All those management courses and leadership development weekends, they didn't count for shit in a real crisis —

Bang! Bang! Bang!

The gunshots echoed down the shaft of the stairwell, booming off the thick concrete walls. Chris yelped in fear, started backing down the stairs.

"Don't move!" hissed Meloy. He hugged the shadows, torch extinguished, neck craned upwards, baton in hand. "Shots fired. Sounds like it's coming from the main lobby."

"We need to get back to the SOR," Chris whispered.

Meloy shook his head. "We go up."

Chris couldn't believe his ears. "Are you stupid? That's gunfire, Mark. Real guns, real bullets. We're going back down, wait for the appropriate response teams. That's a direct order."

Meloy's face wrinkled with contempt. "I'm going up and you're coming with me. You can hide behind your desk later."

"How dare you!"

"You can write me up if it makes you feel any better, but right now there might be people up there who need our help."

Chris fumed, knowing Meloy would write his own report, paint Chris in a bad light. But going up, putting himself in harm's way, was simply out of the question. He pointed to the emergency door between them. "We can get out this way, make our way through the car park."

Meloy shook his head. "You smell that? That's smoke, petrol, vehicle fires, probably. Opening that door could suffocate us. Too dangerous. We're going up," he ordered.

"Don't force me to pull rank — "

"No arguments," Meloy growled. "Draw your baton and follow me. Try and act like a police officer for once in your career."

"You can't speak to me like that," Chris hissed. "I'll have your warrant card."

"Do what you like. In the meantime, you're going up and getting stuck in."

"No. We go through the car park," Chris insisted, almost stamping his foot. It was the smart move, couldn't Meloy see that? Walking out into a wide-open lobby, probably into gunfire, was plain stupid. The car park, with its shadows and concrete pillars, that was the better option.

"Are you deaf? Can't you feel the heat on the other side of that door?" Meloy said. "C'mon, we're wasting time."

"I'm giving you a direct order," Chris snapped. "Now follow me." He reached for the emergency release handle.

"Don't touch that fucking door!"

Meloy scrambled towards him but Chris was determined. The last thing he felt was the heat running through the metal handle just as he cracked the door open —

A pressurised ball of flame punched the door into Chris' face, knocking him on his backside and saving his life. Meloy was engulfed, alight from head to toe, a staggering, screaming roman candle of melted hair, clothing and flesh. Chris screamed too, scrambling away from the blackened creature that cannoned off the concrete walls, its arms extended like some charred Frankenstein's monster. Then Meloy switched direction and hit the handrail. He toppled over and plummeted down the shaft, screaming all the way.

The bone-crunching impact of his body hitting the concrete floor below cut off that terrible sound.

The heat wrapped itself around Chris like a thick blanket. He felt something warm and wet on his face. Blood, from a small cut under his hairline. He started coughing, the smoke thick, black and choking, filling the stairwell fast as it acted like a chimney. He dragged himself to his feet and peered over the railing, but all he could see was a small fire far below. It was Meloy, obviously, but Chris wasn't going to go down there. Instead, he stared past the flames into the car park. Only the cars closest to the door were alight, maybe a dozen or so. Beyond them, through the thick curtain of smoke, daylight.

The smoke-filled chamber would be his excuse, the terrible death of his subordinate confirmation of his lucky escape. As for his colleagues in the SOR, well, they'd probably be okay. Probably.

He took a deep breath and plunged through the door, hugging the wall to his right. He felt the heat of the flames, saw a wide gap between the vehicles and ran for it. Then he was through, out into the main car park and fresh air. He crouched behind an undamaged car, panting, searching the immediate area. No one had seen him. He smeared blood across his face, his neck. He rolled across the dirty concrete, his face and uniform now a costume, a badge of courage for those that might wonder why the head of the SOR had deserted his post.

He peered through the vehicle window. There was no one to be seen, the burning cars behind him belching thick black smoke that rolled up the ramp and out into the evening air.

The ramp.

That would be Chris' way out. Up on the street, he

would find other officers, support units, a cordon, a melee of reporters with their long lenses. Law and order would be waiting, and perhaps one of those waiting photographers would snap an iconic photograph of a blood-soaked police officer emerging from the scene of the terror attack, striding bravely towards his colleagues.

Towards safety.

Because right now, it was the only thing that Chris Hunt cared about.

THE HERON TOWER
CITY OF LONDON

Five hundred and forty-six feet.

That's how far below her the pavement was, and the only reason Salma Nawaz wasn't already falling towards it was the few millimetres of toughened glass she was pinned against was still holding. But it wouldn't last. And that's why Salma was rapidly losing her mind.

The thirty-four-year-old IT Service Manager pushed and clawed against the unyielding mass of shouting, screaming bodies that had her pinned against the full-length windows of the forty-second floor, but it was hopeless. Her body was crushed against the glass, her neck twisted in pain, her lungs fighting for air. The view beyond the window, of chaotic streets and columns of thick smoke, only fuelled her terror. She looked up instead, saw her palms pressed against the glass, her watch face, the minutes ticking away towards the bottom of the hour. How could the world fall apart so quickly?

At six pm, Salma had been sat in a meeting room one floor down from her desk at Lewison Butler, the prestigious financial clearing house where she worked. She'd been pretending to listen to what was being said around the table, nodding thoughtfully at the right moments, making notes on the pad in her lap. Doodling, in fact, because Salma was bored and wanted to get out of there as soon as possible. Why did people have to call meetings so late? Didn't they have lives, homes to go to? So, it was a relief when the lights went out and the slide deck presentation vanished from the whiteboard.

"That's odd," someone said.

"I need to get going anyway," a senior manager declared, looking at his watch and getting to his feet. "I suggest we pick this up tomorrow."

It was the signal most were waiting for, and everybody headed for the door. They filed outside, and Salma veered towards the staircase. She was halfway up to the next floor when she heard the scream.

She stopped on the landing and listened. The scream faded fast, echoing off the walls. Very carefully, Salma peeked over the handrail. The stairs switched back for hundreds of feet below her, silent, ominous, and then her vertigo kicked in and she stepped back. A very low *boom* reverberated through the stairwell. Salma felt her heart beat a little faster. Something was going on.

When she stepped out onto the forty-second floor the first thing she noticed was the gloom. The ceiling lights had failed, and every desk was empty, every computer screen lifeless. Then she heard another scream, louder, closer.

It startled her, but almost immediately the scream was drowned out by a chorus of panicked shouts. There was some sort of commotion coming from the other side of the building. The floor she was on was huge, open-plan, wrapped around a central hub of elevators, storerooms, kitchens and two staircases. She turned right, then right again. *There.*

A crowd had gathered at the east-facing windows, blotting out the light. What on earth were they looking at? Salma didn't want to get too close; heights frightened her, something she kept to herself, happy that her desk was situated well away from the wall of glass that wrapped itself around the forty-second floor. During orientation, she'd been informed that the windows and frames were of the highest safety standards, could withstand thousands of pounds of pressure and were practically unbreakable, but none of that was any consolation to Salma. The only statistic she remembered was that here, on the forty-second floor, she was standing five hundred and forty-six feet above the streets of London. And that thought alone unsettled her.

And yet she felt drawn to the crowd, the windows beyond. There were maybe a hundred people gathered there, looking out over the sprawl of East London. Some were shouting, pointing, but Salma couldn't understand what they were saying. What on earth was going on?

And then someone bolted, barrelling past her. She caught a glimpse of the man, one of the server team, his face ashen. Several others broke away, scrambling for the staircase. Now Salma was really scared, but the lure of the unknown drew her closer. She was short, only five-three, and could barely see over the heads around her, so she climbed up onto a desk and peered over the crowd.

The scream rose in her throat. She slapped a hand over her mouth.

A short distance away, and roughly the same altitude, a giant airliner circled the sky, two of its engines trailing black smoke. Salma watched in horrified fascination as the aircraft banked sharply and headed towards the city.

Towards their building.

A dozen more people broke away and bolted for the stairs. Salma wanted to run after them, but her legs felt like water, her feet rooted to the desk, her eyes transfixed by the monstrous spectacle that was drawing ever closer. Without thinking, Salma jumped off the desk and pushed her way to the window. It was an Air France Airbus, one of those huge double-decker things, a five-hundred seater. The pilot was clearly fighting for control as the wings dipped and swayed, and the aircraft yawed from side to side. Salma saw that the tail fin was also damaged, the upper half shattered and blackened, trailing ribbons of twisted aluminium. She could only imagine the terror of the passengers inside as their aircraft lost height over the city. The Airbus loomed, the sound of its screaming engines piercing the thick glass.

It was almost upon them.

One moment it seemed far away but then the office darkened further as the huge airliner filled the sky in front of the building. Seconds later it thundered past, the wingtip barely fifty feet from where Salma stood. In its wake, the whole building shook to its foundations. Pictures sprang off the walls and everything rattled violently. The crowd scattered, desperate to see the plane's demise. It was only then that Salma realised people were actually filming the unfolding event on their phones.

She followed them anyway, across the floor to the west-facing windows, where even more people had gathered to witness the terrible deaths of so many. Salma felt sick, ashamed, yet unable to drag her eyes away from the doomed aircraft. She flinched as a wing suddenly exploded in a puff of fire and black smoke, and then the Airbus twisted in the sky, plunging nose first towards the ground. Salma watched it all the way, transfixed. It disappeared into a cluster of buildings and a giant fireball roiled and mushroomed into the air, the explosion rumbling across the city.

Thousands had just died, Salma realised. Nausea made her head swim.

"What the fuck is happening?" someone behind her shouted.

"Look at the fires, all over the city!"

"It's terrorists. Jihadis," another voice blurted. "We should all get the fuck out of here."

"We should stay put. It's safer."

"Suit yourself. The next plane might not miss."

People were fleeing en masse now, and Salma stumbled away from the window. She had to get her things, get home as soon as possible. To safety.

She pushed and shoved her way through the crowd, grabbed her handbag from beneath her desk, her summer raincoat from the stand. She didn't know whether to wear it or throw it over her arm. *Get out!* her inner voice commanded. She threw the coat on her desk and ran for the stairs.

Before she'd made it halfway, the door slammed open and a tide of people spilled out into the office, shouting and screaming, tumbling over desks and sprawling onto the carpeted floor. Salma watched in horror as one woman lost her footing and went under the crowd. She tried to get up but someone trod on her face and then someone else fell on top of her and she was lost under the mob.

And then she saw them, chasing the crowd onto the forty-second, the men with knives and machetes, hacking and stabbing at the fallen. There were six of them, maybe more, their weapons taped to their hands, their screams of hate reverberating across the floor. Salma watched as one of them straddled the fallen woman, plunging the knife into her neck and face as if he were preparing a microwave meal. She screamed, the noise cut off as one of his blades went through her throat. She made a terrible gurgling sound, and then her attacker was up again, slashing at another runner.

Salma turned and sprinted away. She had no idea where she was going but thought that if she circled the entire floor she could get in behind the attackers and make the stairs. She was operating on instinct now, leaping over bodies, dodging between desks and scattered chairs. Screams of terror, of pain and rage, filled the air. She didn't look back, just kept moving.

She didn't see the overturned chair until she collided with it. She felt the bone in her shin snap, put her hands out to break her fall. She hit the ground hard and screamed in pain.

Then she panicked. No one was stopping to help, just leaping over her like some macabre Grand National. She hauled herself to her feet, hobbled as fast as she could, the pain shooting through her leg and hip like hot needles.

She slowed, looking for a place to hide. Over her shoulder, through the glass wall of a meeting room, she saw two of the terrorists stabbing Tom Phillips to death. Tom was a database engineer, a family man, gentle, funny, and very overweight. Now he was swatting feebly at his attackers, screaming for mercy as they stabbed him again and again in his arms and stomach. She watched him as he slid down the wall, no longer able to defend himself. His attackers never stopped, just kept sinking their blades into his blood-soaked shirt.

"Salma! Over here!"

She turned, almost sobbed with relief. Ellie from Service Delivery was beckoning her from a doorway, one of the many storerooms dotted across the floor. With all her strength, she stood up and scrambled over there. Ellie caught her, helped her towards the window at the back of the room. Salma sat down against it, her fear of heights no longer relevant. She was breathless, terrified and in severe pain.

"Lock the door, Ellie!"

"There's no lock."

"Then barricade it somehow."

"We've got to help the others," Ellie said.

"They just killed Tom Phillips, butchered him right in front of me. They'll kill us all!"

"Calm down," Ellie told her. "We've got to help the others. There's plenty of room in here."

Before Salma could argue Ellie was at the door, beckoning others towards the small room. In less than a minute it was filled with bodies, all squeezing into the cramped space. Salma dragged herself to her feet, hopped onto the window ledge to avoid getting trampled. Everyone was scared. Salma, now disabled and in severe pain, was terrified.

"Shut the fucking door!" an unseen man hissed.

"Wait, there're others out there — "

"Close it," a woman cried. "They're right behind us!"

"No!" Ellie cried, and then Salma screamed. Two of the attackers were already at the door, shoving their way inside. It was a space that could hold barely ten people. Salma reckoned there were at least twenty of them squeezed in there. Ellie, trying to push against the door, was the first to die as an arm reached around the door and stabbed her in the eye, then her neck. Blood sprayed over those closest to her. They screamed and shouted, surged backwards, squeezing the mass of bodies behind them. Salma's head cannoned off the window. Her vision swam. She fought to keep her weight on her good foot as the bodies closed in around her. The screaming was horrendous, the wails of the stabbed, the dying, shredding her nerves. Salma couldn't look, clamped her hands over her ears. That's when she heard it, or rather, felt it.

An audible crack.

She twisted her face upwards and her blood froze. There. A small fissure had appeared at the top of the huge glass pane and as she watched, the jagged finger reached down towards her. Maybe it was the plane, the near miss that had somehow weakened it. Now people were pushing backwards, desperate to escape the slashing, stabbing terrorists who had them trapped like rats.

Salma tried to turn her body, but she was pinned fast by the writhing, screaming mass against her. Her chest hurt and it was getting difficult to breathe. The crack had worked its way down to her fingertips, and a fine shower of dust and plaster began to rain down on her head. With every ounce of strength she possessed, Salma tried to wriggle her way out, but the wall of bodies pressing against her, against her broken leg, had her firmly trapped. The attackers were shouting, screaming bloody jihad as they carved their way further into the wall of bodies. Men and women screamed. The survivors pushed harder, crushing Salma against the glass.

"No! Please! Stop it! Stop it!"

The top of the window was suddenly wrenched out of its concrete housing, the thick pane tilting outwards a few degrees. It held there as air from outside rushed in, swirling around the narrow room.

The screaming intensified.

Tears streamed down Salma's face. Her broken shin was causing her agony, but still, she tried to wriggle away from the window, knowing that it would only push her closer to the murderers behind her. But it was no use. Salma knew she was about to die, one way or the other. She gave up then, let her body slump against the cool glass, felt the wind against her face, against her outstretched fingers. Close behind her, she could hear the shouts, the screams, the pleading, the grunting of murderous effort, the terrible cries of the wounded, the dying. Salma didn't want to hear anything anymore, didn't want to wait for her turn to be skewered like an animal, by animals. She wanted to be free.

The window shuddered, tilted further. Concrete crumbled and rained down onto her hair, her face. She pushed against the glass, felt the crush behind her, lending their own weight. There was a loud crack and Salma closed her eyes.

And suddenly she was free, tumbling through the air, her scream mingling with the others around her, their awful chorus of imminent death echoing through the financial heart of the city.

Five hundred and forty-six feet.

It was her last conscious thought as Salma Nawaz's body slammed into the pavement at terminal velocity.

There was no cordon to be seen when Chris Hunt made it to street level, no marked cars or police vans choking the roads, no army of gun-wielding officers or command vehicles, and certainly no photographers.

Instead, there was chaos: smashed shop fronts, burning cars and bodies. There were lots of bodies.

Some were police, but mostly they were civilians, twenty or thirty perhaps, men, women and children, spread out across the road. Some were bloodless and intact and looked like they were sleeping. Others were bloodied and mangled, their clothes filthy, as if they'd been run over. Which they probably had, Chris guessed. That's how these things normally started.

Gunfire rang out, ringing off the buildings around him. Chris was terrified. He cowered behind an abandoned security hut, heart pounding in his chest. Beyond the security fence, an armed response vehicle had mounted the pavement, its windscreen and bodywork peppered with bullet holes. The driver and the passenger were dead, that much

Chris could see, eyes wide and mouths open, their faces caked in blood. Every police officer was a target.

Chris swallowed hard and yanked open the door to the hut. He ducked inside and began stripping off his stab vest and utility belt. Handcuffs and CS spray were useless anyway. He grabbed a dark waterproof coat hanging behind the door and pulled it on, but not before he threw his police epaulettes in the bin. He zipped it up to cover his white police shirt, making him feel like less of a target. But he couldn't stay there. He had to find safety, fast.

He heard a siren and ducked outside. The wailing got closer, a vehicle somewhere on Victoria Street maybe. Chris used the sound as cover, yanking open the pedestrian security gate and stepping out onto the street. He was about to run across the road but stopped. He crouched down by the ARV, reached inside and retrieved one of the dead officers' handguns. It was a Glock 17, heavy and wet with blood. Chris kept his fingers away from the pressure-trigger and jammed it into his coat pocket. He wasn't an expert on guns but he'd taken the firearms prelim course, hoping it would improve his chances for promotion. He'd failed, and he still resented the instructors for that decision. He'd played the gay card too, to no avail. Still, having a weapon made him feel safer.

He moved to the corner of the street, looked carefully in both directions. In the distance, the junction with Victoria Street lay abandoned, the storefronts darkened, the traffic lights dead. In the other direction, the Transport for London building loomed above the street, squatting above St James' Park tube station. Chris had been there many times for meetings with his transport police counterparts. They had an operations room there, manned twenty-four seven. He knew the layout reasonably well too. His chances of finding safety were looking better already.

He pulled the gun from his pocket, cringing at the stickiness of the blood-soaked grip. He checked the magazine, cocked the weapon. He didn't want to use it but it would serve as a deterrent should anyone confront him.

A volley of shots startled him, his head spinning left and right as the sound bounced around the tall buildings. Probably the army barracks opposite St James' Park, he thought, judging by the sheer number of rounds being fired. Maybe they were under attack, or maybe they were deploying out onto the street. Chris thought that one through; his clothes were dark and he was carrying a gun. If some Neanderthal, trigger-happy squaddie saw him he might get shot at. He shoved the gun back in his pocket and took one last look around.

Clear.

He pushed himself up and sprinted across the road. From the corner of his eye, he caught a movement to his left. A hundred metres away a man stepped out from behind a vehicle on Caxton Street holding a rifle.

"Shit!"

Chris made it across the road just as the first shots rang out. He kept going, charging towards the entrance to the TFL building. He slowed as he reached the doors. The large reception area was empty, dark and lifeless. Chris looked over his shoulder. The man with the rifle would be right behind him. Beyond the glass door, he saw a cone of light sweep across the walls. He thumped on the glass and a black security guard poked his head around the corner, saw him. Chris waved his warrant card.

"Open the door! Quickly!"

The guard did as instructed, unbolting the door top and bottom. Chris barged past him.

"Lock it! There's a gunman right behind me!" He made for the stairs, waited for the guard on the first-floor landing. "Where are the police?"

The security guard shrugged. "Someone said a plane crashed near Oxford Street."

"I mean the transport police. Where are they?"

The man's eyes were wide saucers of fear, and sweat glistened on his ebony face. "There were bombs at Victoria, one on the tube, the other on a train in the station. Many dead. They all leave."

"Don't let anyone else in," Chris told him. "They could be a terrorist. The police will be here soon."

He charged up the stairs before the man could respond. So, if the transport police had left the building it was pointless trying to find sanctuary with them. Time for plan B.

The TFL complex was a warren of corridors built around four large wings with a multitude of annexes and offices. It was after seven pm now, and the building would be mostly empty. He would find somewhere, a room with a window and places to hide, and barricade himself in until the crisis was over. A few hours maybe, by dawn at the latest.

Outside the gunfire sounded like it was intensifying. Then the thought came to him; this building had a roof terrace. He'd had a coffee up there once, during a break from some equality conference or something. Tenth floor. Or was it the twelfth? In any case, the view would give him a much clearer picture of what was happening, and perhaps where the security cordons had been set up. He could probably map a route to safety from up there.

He headed for the main staircase, climbed it cautiously

until he reached the top floor. He made his way slowly and quietly along the corridors, following the signs to the roof. Halfway down one such passageway Chris heard voices and stopped. He heard sobbing behind a door and leaned closer to listen. Suddenly it swung inwards.

Chris jumped, as did the man who opened the door. Behind him, there maybe a dozen people, men and women, sat on chairs in the middle of a large, open-plan office. One or two of the women were crying, their colleagues gathered around, trying to console them. The men were ashen-faced and scared. The man by the door was in his fifties, balding, and wore a grey suit. He looked relieved.

"Thank God," he puffed, then turned around and addressed the group. "It's okay everyone, the police have arrived."

"Be quiet," hissed Chris, pushing past the man and closing the door quickly. "How d'you know I'm police?"

The man pointed. "You all wear the same trousers and boots."

Of course we do, Chris realised. *And if this moron can spot it, anyone can.* "What are you all doing up here?"

"Taking shelter of course," the man said as if explaining to a child. "Sounds like a bloody war going on out there. What's happening?"

Chris ignored him and marched over to the windows. They were sealed, and there was little to be seen, other than huge columns of smoke that were blocking out the sun. The glass vibrated with the rattle of gunfire. He flinched, realising how stupid it was to stand near the window. He headed back across the room. On the way, he snatched at a telephone on a desk, punched a couple of buttons. Dead.

"What shall we do?" a sour-faced woman asked him as

he walked past. Chris ignored her. Grey suit blocked his path.

"Look, we need some help here. You're a policeman. Tell us what to do."

Chris looked at the faces around him and saw only fear and panic. He had to tell them something if only to get this arsehole off his back.

"Help is on its way," he lied. "In the meantime, there's a water cooler over there, and you've got the loos, so your immediate needs are catered for. Stay away from the doors and windows and try to keep as quiet as possible."

"That's it? That's all you've got?" sneered one of the younger men, a working-class type in jeans, trainers and a designer top. "What if we run out of bog roll? Or tea bags? What do we do then?"

Chris felt his cheeks burning. He wasn't used to being challenged, especially by oiks like this one.

"Just remain where you are. Help is coming."

He left the room, slammed the door behind him before the smart arse could say anything else. He turned a corner and daylight flooded the corridor. He pushed open the glass doors to the terrace.

The noise hit him like a wave, the roar of automatic weapons fire, loud detonations, glass shattering, shouting, screaming, all pin-balling off the surrounding buildings. Chris stayed low all the way to the perimeter wall, then swivelled his head to get his bearings. The Ministry of Justice building loomed across the street. It looked unscathed at first, but a closer inspection revealed fires in the lobby and thick black smoke billowing across the road below. Higher up, more smoke funnelled out of broken windows. There were people up there too, he saw. Several had spotted him and were waving frantically. Chris pretended not to see them. There was nothing he could do anyway.

He looked east towards Parliament Square. He couldn't see the square itself but he saw tiny figures running in that direction. There were bodies lying on the road, and several tourist coaches were burning furiously. Somewhere over Whitehall, a huge pillar of black smoke towered into the sky.

A low rumble reached his ears, getting louder with every second. Then he saw them, approaching from the southeast. They were moving fast, so fast that by the time he recognised them as fighter jets they were already thundering low overhead, the noise so terrifying that Chris wailed and jammed his hands against his ears. And then they were gone, thundering away across the city, spitting out flares in their wake.

Chris felt sick, his legs suddenly weak. He sat down, slumping heavily against the terrace wall. This wasn't a terrorist incident; this was a war, some sort of revolution, a coup perhaps. Truth was he had no idea who might —

The bullet cracked off the brickwork close to his right shoulder. Chris rolled away, scrambled to his feet, an involuntary sob belching from his mouth. He made it into the corridor just as another round zipped past, tearing a chunk out of the wall in front of him. He ducked around the corner, stopping to catch his breath. *A sniper, just randomly shooting people.* Chris' head spun. This was utter madness.

"You alright?"

It was grey suit, peering around the office door.

"Don't go out there," Chris warned. "There's a sniper."

He heard the word *sniper* pass beyond the door, a whispering infection of terror. The sobbing started again.

"You'd better stay with us," grey suit told him.

"No, I have to find my colleagues."

The oik pushed his way past the door, stood in front of Chris. "*Help's on its way*; that's what you said. Just a bunch of bullshit, right? To keep us sweet?" He looked Chris up and down. "Take a look outside, pal. Dead coppers all over the place. You want to end up like them? Don't be a mug. You're better off here, with us."

"I can't. I have to find my colleagues."

Chris pushed past him, heading back to the main staircase.

"Don't be a bloody idiot," grey suit shouted after him, but Chris was already through the doors and heading back down the stairs. One of the annexes would suffice. He'd find a storeroom, a stationary cupboard, hole up, stay hidden until —

The gunfire was deafening and suddenly very close.

Chris stopped dead. He heard shouting below, so he inched towards the handrail and peered over. Down in the lobby, he saw the black security guard, pleading with three Asian men in jeans and t-shirts. All of them were heavily armed, with black IS scarves wrapped around their heads. Chris' blood ran cold. As he watched, one of the men ran a vicious-looking knife across the guard's throat. The man staggered backwards, his hands trying to stem the flow of blood that spilled over his hands. He hit the wall and slid down it, those wide eyes full of pain and fear.

Chris turned and ran back up the stairs. He had to get out of the building before more terrorists turned up and started moving through the corridors. If they were murdering people in uniform that easily, Chris wouldn't stand a chance, no matter how many mosques he'd visited. But where to go?

Whitehall seemed the obvious answer. It wasn't far

away, and safety would lie behind the security gates of Parliament Square. He could be there in under ten minutes. It would mean exposing himself to the multitude of dangers out on the street, but what choice did he have? He could either stay here, try and find a hiding place until help arrived – *if* help arrived – or be discovered in the meantime. No, he had to get away, he decided. Anything else was suicide.

He found a fire exit at the other end of the building – a narrow, deserted stairwell. He pulled the gun from his coat pocket, ignored the blood and gripped it tight. He moved downstairs quickly, his hand squeaking on the handrail. When he reached the ground floor he paused by the exit door, heard the sound of gunfire outside. It was coming from the army barracks, Chris was sure of that. He slapped at the door release bar and inched it open a crack. Parked cars were ablaze everywhere, and thick smoke hung like a black curtain across the street, teased by the evening breeze. The smoke swirled and eddied, and Chris saw the empty road opposite. A potential escape route.

A door slammed high above. Chris heard shouting, then harsh whispers, then footsteps. Whoever was up there they were coming down towards him. Could be friend, but more likely foe. Chris wasn't about to take any chances.

He took a deep breath, barged open the door and ran across the street.

Fear snapped at his heels.

He was out of shape, breathless within seconds. His heart beat loudly in his ears as his boots pounded the asphalt, black smoke swirling around him. He ran past the Ministry of Justice building and suddenly he was in clear air. He swung right into Queen Anne's Gate, an elegant street of Regency period buildings, the northern row of which backed onto Birdcage Walk and St James' Park. Despite its proximity to the nearby violence, the street appeared to be a quiet, secluded oasis of calm.

Chris didn't stop running until he was halfway along it. Then he threw himself behind a parked car, exhausted, his breath coming in heaving, wheezing sobs. He lay on his stomach for several minutes, peering beneath the cars, ready to drag himself beneath one should any terrorists come his way. The street appeared completely untouched by the fighting, marred only by drifting debris: the multitude of paper that scratched and tumbled along the street; the smouldering, burning ash and embers that drifted and spiralled from the sky. There didn't seem to be anyone else around, nobody on foot or any vehicular activity. When his lungs stopped heaving, Chris decided he'd head towards Birdcage Walk, then Whitehall. And safety.

He was about to get to his feet when Chris heard a shout ahead of him. He crouched low and peered through the car window, the pistol tight in his hand.

Fuck!

There were three armed men heading in his direction, far enough away that they wouldn't see him if he moved, but where would he go? He couldn't head back the way he'd come, and he certainly wasn't going to engage them. No, he would hide. Yet what troubled him was the apparent confidence of these terrorists, heading towards battle as if they owned the place, walking along the middle of the street as if they'd already declared victory —

Oh no.

Chris' hand shook, the Glock rattling quietly. Was Whitehall gone? Downing Street too? They were coming from that direction, walking with confidence, their weapons held loosely in their hands. He heard another shout, and the approaching men swung around. Chris was horrified to see more terrorists jogging after them, then embracing each other. He heard English spoken, and then they fanned out across the street, picking up their pace as they headed towards the battle at the barracks. There was now a dozen of them, moving tactically, checking cars, aiming their weapons up at the windows of the houses as they passed. Chris wanted to urinate badly. They were going to find him, question him, then kill him. Everything was moving too fast, spinning out of control —

Tap. Tap. Tap.

At first, he thought it was his imagination. His ears were still ringing from the gunfire and he tried to ignore it, but it was persistent.

Tap. Tap. Tap.

He turned around and found himself staring down at an elderly man, his smiling face peering up at him from behind a basement flat window. He was tapping on the glass, gesturing towards the gleaming black front door at the foot of the stairs. Chris checked on the approaching terrorists. They were getting closer. Their blood would be up, their trigger fingers itchy. It was a no-brainer.

Chris crawled across the pavement, his shins bouncing painfully off the stone steps that led down to the basement. The heavy black door swung open and Chris dragged himself inside. The door closed behind him and he staggered to his feet, breathing hard.

The smartly-dressed man who stood before him was in his late seventies, his snow-white hair immaculately parted to one side and his thin lips curling upwards into a broad smile. He held out his hand.

"Are you alright, old chap? Looks frightfully dangerous out there."

THE MISSILES
EUROPE

WHILE EUROPE REELED UNDER THE INITIAL ASSAULTS, IS missile teams across the Islamic crescent carried out their final pre-flight checks. Satisfied that the birds were fully fuelled and armed, they waited patiently for the launch order. They didn't have long to wait.

From locations too numerous to count, hundreds of AGM-200C TSSAM Super Cruise missiles rocketed into the air. The launch points were varied: assault ships at sea in the Mediterranean, silos deep in the desert, ground-launch trucks in the Bosnian and Turkish Hills, and IS military aircraft cruising thousands of feet above the North African coast. The missiles roared into the evening sky, their highly-advanced engines trimming power and levelling off. That's when the computers went to work.

Pre-programmed with specific data, the advanced target processing chips cross-referenced it with complex on-board guidance systems and made the necessary course adjustments. At fourteen feet long, the Super Cruise was a small weapon, but it was extremely powerful and infinitely more accurate than its twentieth-century predecessor, its design specifications smuggled out of the Raytheon labs in Texas by agents sympathetic to the idea of a global Caliphate and corrupted by the lure of a bulging offshore account. After years of testing, Caliphate technicians had developed a near-exact replica of the American-made missile. And they planned to make full use of its devastating capabilities.

After achieving optimal cruising speed, the missiles switched to attack mode, adjusting their fins and dropping altitude to approximately ninety feet. The solid fuel-cell engines punched the missiles forward, accelerating to over six hundred miles per hour, making tiny course corrections every quarter second. Terrain Mapping Systems and Forward Look-down InfraRed cameras constantly scanned the horizon for obstacles and made adjustments where necessary, all the while closing distance to target.

In southern Europe, the Super Cruise missiles began to answer the insistent calls of the targeting transponders planted at airfields, military headquarters buildings, airfields, communications centres, tank and armour sheds, marine and naval bases, and hundreds of other strategic locations across the continent. The initial wave of missiles finally reached their targets, dipping their noses and accelerating with a final surge of power. The Super Cruise was accurate to within twenty feet and as the missiles rained down all over Europe, the results were devastating. Explosions rippled across the continent, damaging or destroying their targets as planned. Only four missiles malfunctioned and never made their final destinations. It mattered not.

The firestorm had begun.

"Sir, you need to keep your fucking head down!"

Terry McAuliffe, U.S. Ambassador to the Court of St James, struggled to breathe as the Gunny's hand shoved his face into the carpet. Pressing on his back and legs, a suffocating mound of uniforms, all weighed down by Kevlar, all trying to protect him from incoming. He'd been in that same position for over a minute and it was becoming extremely uncomfortable. He struggled beneath them, and Gunnery Sergeant Perry grabbed his neck and jammed his head back into the carpet.

"Stay the fuck down!"

McAuliffe was tired of being protected. Above the deafening explosions and the rattle of automatic gunfire, McAuliffe yelled in Perry's face.

"Back off, Gunny! That's an order!"

Perry saw the look in McAuliffe's eyes and relented. "Fine, but stay low for Christ's sake."

No shit, McAuliffe wanted to tell him. It was common knowledge that McAuliffe was an Iraq War vet, a platoon commander with the 82nd Airborne, a man who'd seen some serious fighting in Fallujah, a battle that had earned him a citation, a Purple Heart and a butt-full of grenade shrapnel. McAuliffe had known rough times, that was for sure. What riled him was being treated like some kind of newbie, but he understood. His safety was in the hands of the men around him, first and foremost. Not theirs, his. He had to remember that.

He flinched as heavy-calibre rounds began punching fist-sized holes through the walls of the embassy building. They might be in one the world's major cities but in the last hour London had descended into a combat zone and it didn't look like the cavalry was coming to the rescue. All comms were down, the power out, and the embassy was under assault from all sides. The situation was becoming increasingly untenable, and the thought crossed McAuliffe's mind that he might not make it out alive. If that was the case, well, so be it. Like the Marines around him, he'd go down fighting.

The trousers of his tuxedo were shredded at the knees, his once-white shirt now caked in dust and blood. McAuliffe's mind fought to catch up. How did this happen so fast? Without any warning? He'd been working in his third-floor office only a few minutes ago...

...HUNCHED OVER HIS LAPTOP, TAPPING AWAY AT THE keyboard, preparing some last-minute notes before his evening engagement. His speech an important one, a precursor to a new trade initiative that had quietly given Beecham and his beleaguered government hope of a boost to their economic position. What the Brits didn't know was that the UK was about to become America's first partner in a new era of friendship and economic prosperity, and when the Brits were made privy to the finer points of that deal, well, to put it bluntly, they'd shit a brick.

Because things were about to change.

Once again, America was about to reshape the world, and not before time. After 9/11 her reputation had been trampled in the bloody quagmires of Iraq and Afghanistan, the enemy body count rising faster than a Baghdad thermometer. The whole world knew that elements behind the Bush administration had falsified the intelligence, a crime that had cost the lives of how many people? A million? Two? It was worse than tragic.

So, for the last few years America had retreated from the field of perpetual conflict, no longer willing to interfere in the business of others, no more dictating policy, no more gunship diplomacy: a nation focused on its own well-being and that of its people. She was still a superpower, more so now than ever before, but the global perception of America was about to undergo a fundamental shift. She was to become a force for good, for all of mankind, period. The world was about to change, and everyone needed to be onboard.

McAuliffe paused, fingers hovering over his keyboard.

The stumbling block would be the Middle East of course. Islam had a long memory, the ambassador knew. Despite the sudden rise of Wazir's Islamic State, the dissolution of old borders, the fusing together of former disparate territories, Wazir continued to feed his people a diet of disaffection, that the world was against them, their religion under constant attack, that everywhere Islam took root it sowed mistrust and hatred amongst others. That message went global, his weekly address beamed live across the world.

McAuliffe knew the message was fake news. Since its

explosion across the Arabian Peninsula almost fifteen hundred years ago, Islam had never assimilated or fostered a peaceful co-existence. It displaced. It spread. It conquered. The Qur'an was a literal text, not open for reinterpretation or reformation, and its adherents were bound by Sharia under pain of punishment and death. That was the truth, as stark and as disturbing as it was. And as the geopolitical map shifted after 9/11, Islam spread quickly across Africa and Europe, triggering local conflicts, wider political instability, a toppling of the dominoes across North Africa. But they didn't stop there, on the shores of the Mediterranean.

Thanks to Europe's historic self-loathing and progressive policies, its capitals were now ringed by Muslim enclaves, its crumbling suburbs now simmering ghettos, its streets the new battleground for never-ending terror attacks. The same was true of the UK, McAuliffe knew, its burgeoning population fuelled by an unwillingness to control its own borders, a well-meaning but suicidal political correctness, a string of governments blinded to the dangers of an unbending ideology that sought not to spread a message of peace but to conquer. His great-grandfather had spent a year in England back in 1943, before hitting the French beaches on D-Day the following June. McAuliffe knew that the England of today would be unrecognisable to the old guy.

And that's when the lights went out.

McAuliffe clicked his desk lamp a couple of times, noticed the overheads were out too. He'd picked up the phone. Dead. His private secretary, Carol, entered the room.

"You too, sir?"

"Any idea what's happening?"

He registered the flash a split second before the loudest

explosion he'd ever heard shook the building and threw him to the floor. He scrambled beneath his desk as ceiling tiles and light fittings crashed around him.

Carol was on her hands and knees in the doorway, her hair caked in plaster. She screamed as gunfire erupted outside and several rounds smacked off the ballistic glass behind McAuliffe's desk. *Bomb,* McAuliffe knew. He rolled out from under his desk and helped his secretary to her feet.

"You okay, Carol?"

As Carol coughed and spluttered, the sound of gunfire grew louder, and rounds rattled off the building like a sudden, violent rainstorm. The windows of his corner office were already cracked and splintered, the protective scrim covering – the external panels that gave the embassy its distinctive look – blown away.

"Get everyone down to the basement shelter, nice and orderly please, Carol." As he said the words another blast shook the building. McAuliffe grabbed his assistant by the arm and practically dragged her into the outer office.

"Move. Fast as you can."

As Carol bolted from the room, three men in combat uniform appeared in the doorway. One of them was Major Peter Vincenzo, head of the embassy Marine detachment, accompanied by two escorts, all of them armed. Vincenzo saw McAuliffe, beckoned him to follow.

"Let's go, Mister Ambassador!"

Without preamble, the two escorting Marines grabbed McAuliffe by the arms and propelled him into the corridor outside. Embassy staff ran past them towards the emergency staircase, and red lights throbbed along the ceiling. As they ran past a bank of elevators, McAuliffe thought he heard someone hammering from inside.

"Wait, I think there's — "

"No time," barked Vincenzo over his shoulder.

McAuliffe planted his feet and shook his arms free. "There're people trapped in that elevator," he told the Marine. A throng of civilian staff pushed past them, heading for the open stairwell door that would take them to the basement shelters. "Calmly and quietly, folks," he bellowed after them.

"Upper floors are being evacuated," Vincenzo told him. "I'll get a team to take care of the elevators."

McAuliffe ducked as a succession of smaller explosions rattled the exterior of the building. He heard glass breaking, several shouts and a long piercing scream. The sound of automatic gunfire was relentless.

"What the fuck's happening?" shouted McAuliffe.

"Truck bomb took out the main gate, the Brit cops too," Vincenzo told him. "The outer defence wall is breached and we've got at least thirty armed men inside the perimeter, assaulting the building, half with RPGs and heavy weapons."

RPGs. McAuliffe realised it was an RPG round that had detonated outside his window. One never forgets the sound. "Where's the RSO?"

The Regional Security Officer was McAuliffe's foremost advisor at the embassy, a State Department attache who oversaw every aspect of the embassy's security. He watched Vincenzo shake his head.

"RSO Dodds was inside the gatehouse when the truck blew. There's nothing left."

"Jesus Christ," McAuliffe breathed. "How are we shaping up?"

"Not great. Casualties are mounting and the main entrance lobby is under heavy attack. I got fourteen Marines under my command, and the Diplomatic Security teams make up another dozen or so. Small arms mostly, plus a couple of SAWs. Less than thirty guns and limited ammunition. As long as they don't breach the main building we should be good, that is until help arrives. By now every Brit cop will be on their way here."

McAuliffe gave him a look. "Fucking audacious though, right Pete? I mean, a fully-fledged assault right here, in London? With RPGs?"

"Agreed. Doesn't look or feel like a hit and run, which is why we need to get you to a safe place, and that's down in level four. Time to move, Mister Ambassador."

"Stand fast!"

McAuliffe turned as a voice boomed across the office floor. Ethan Katz, the resident CIA chief, was striding towards them, a ballistic vest covering his normally crisp shirt, an automatic pistol in his hand. With him was another Marine in full combat uniform, his weapon held low, his head swivelling left and right. Katz was strung tight, the Beretta gripped firmly in his hand. He addressed Vincenzo first.

"Major Vee, I need to brief the Ambassador on his evacuation procedures, which means that this building has to be locked down and defended for as long as it takes. I'd be grateful if you would see to that immediately."

Vincenzo held up a hand. "Wait, just back up a minute. This is a terrorist attack, a significant one sure, but you're talking as if — " Vincenzo paused for a moment, saw the look on Katz's face. McAuliffe saw it too.

"Wait, there's something you're not telling us, right Pete?"

Katz nodded, led them both into an alcove that was stacked with boxes of printer paper and office supplies.

Distant voices were ordering everyone to get beneath ground.

"Morning brief said the threat board was clear," McAuliffe reminded the CIA man.

Katz nodded. "Correct, nothing on the local horizon."

"You mean aside from the political marches in support of Wazir's war games, an increase in tension — "

"We're in the UK," Katz reminded him. "It's practically a Wazir outpost most of the time, right Terry?"

"Point taken," McAuliffe relented. "So, what d'you know?"

"Langley called on the sat phone, right after the power went out. Just after the attack began. Reports were coming in thick and fast from across Europe, a lot of it sketchy and uncorroborated, but here's what we do know; combined Turkish and IS forces have invaded Bulgaria, at least twenty tank divisions, all rolling unmolested across the border a short time ago. Athens and Nice are getting pounded by IS naval assets and NORAD detected multiple missile launches originating from across the Caliphate, destination Europe. The power outage we've just experienced? It's not just here in London: every major European city has been hit, and our embassies there are reporting widespread attacks on national government and military buildings. As crazy as it seems, everything is pointing to a major military offensive against Europe by the Islamic State."

"Jesus," whispered McAuliffe.

"Motherfuckers," growled Vincenzo.

"We have to get you out of here," Katz told McAuliffe.

"You want to evacuate the embassy? With all hell breaking loose outside?"

Katz shook his head. "Just you."

"Out of the question," snapped McAuliffe. "I'm staying,

period. How long can they sustain this attack for anyway? Help must be on its way, right? No, we do as Pete says, we follow procedure, get down to the basement. I'm not running out on this embassy or my people, Ethan. That's final."

"Mendes!" Katz called over his shoulder.

A moment later a young Hispanic Marine in full combat gear pushed his way into the alcove. He nodded to McAuliffe. "Sir?"

"Tell him what you saw."

Mendes cleared his throat. "When the first bomb blew, I took a team up onto the roof. We got a tactical observation platform up there, high-powered scopes, thermal imagery, three-sixty degree coverage — "

"Get to the point, son."

Mendes nodded and said, "We've got two observation drones providing real-time footage from the surrounding area. Jihadis are coming in from everywhere, in vehicles, on foot, all getting in on the fight. Must be over a hundred out there already, plus they got shooters in the surrounding buildings. And it's organised, sir, all planned out, no question." Mendes cleared his throat again and said, "While I was up there I saw a passenger jet, a big Airbus, hit the centre of town. It was trailing smoke like it'd been clipped by a missile. There's fire and smoke, all over the city — "

"Including Whitehall," Katz interrupted. "Probably a car or a truck bomb. A lot of gunfire coming from across the river too. This thing isn't sporadic or localised, Terry. It's regional for sure, global, almost definitely. Your safety is paramount. We're getting you out of the embassy."

McAuliffe might've felt overwhelmed but he was a military man, defined by his years of service, the responsibility to his men, his unit, his country. Politicians and civilians evacuate. Soldiers stay and fight. "I'm not leaving, Ethan."

"You're not fucking staying," Katz snapped back. "You want to end up like our guy in Addis Ababa?"

McAuliffe remembered it well, as did much of the world.

Ethiopia, 2023, and rebels had staged a coup that had plunged the country into civil war overnight. Only two navy helicopters had managed to lift US personnel out of the embassy compound before the third was blown out of the air on take-off. The rebels overran the small Marine security detachment before launching a savage, blood-letting spree. Thirty-two Americans were butchered to death, the machete being the Ethiopians' weapon of choice. They saved the Ambassador until last, and they took their time with him. Cut with machetes, he was dragged out into the street before being set upon by a blood-thirsty pack of female rebels and hacked to death. A French TV crew caught the whole event on film and the footage was beamed around the world. Like most Americans, Terry McAuliffe would never forget those terrible images.

Katz put a hand on McAuliffe's shoulder, kept his voice low. "You know the drill, Terry. State Department won't allow another event like that, and frankly neither will any of us here."

"Right," Vincenzo agreed.

"I can't just leave," McAuliffe protested, knowing his pleas were falling on deaf ears. It pained him to think of running while everyone else was left to their fate. The floor shook beneath their feet as another blast rattled the building, forcing McAuliffe to slap a steadying hand against the wall. Dust fell from the ceiling in a fine powder.

"It's not up for discussion," Katz told him. "You're

getting out, that's final. Besides, SecState will have all our asses if we let you ride this thing out." The CIA man turned to Vincenzo. "The only way in is through the main lobby, right?" Vincenzo nodded. "So, hold them there. I don't care what you have to do, just make sure they don't get in."

"We need to initiate burn procedures," McAuliffe said, "destroy all of our intel, classified documents, hard drives, data — "

"Being fried as we speak," Katz assured him.

Vincenzo was already moving when Katz shouted out to him.

"Pete, I'll need some guys for close protection. I'll hang on to Mendes too, send them all back when we're done."

Vincenzo nodded and turned on his heel, making for the stairs. The sound of gunfire seemed suddenly louder.

"This is crazy," McAuliffe said. "There must've been *some* warning, Ethan."

Katz shrugged. "The IS military have been running a constant readiness cycle for years – war games, exercises, you name it, and the Wazir government is constantly agitating against Israel, Tehran, the West. The world has got used to it." He paused for a moment, then said, "Don't tell me you're surprised, Terry. I think we all knew something like this would happen sooner or later."

Before McAuliffe could answer, Mendes was shouting across the office at the four armed Marines who'd spilled out of the west stairwell. They ran over, breathing hard. The one that spoke had a chiselled face and a nose that looked as if it had been broken many times.

"Sir, Gunnery Sergeant Perry. Major Vincenzo sent us up."

"How's it looking down there?" McAuliffe asked.

"The lobby shutters won't hold for much longer," Perry told him.

Katz jabbed a finger. "You've got one job, Gunny, and that's to keep the Ambassador safe until we get him to where he's going. And until we do, I don't want a single hair on his head harmed, got it?"

"Roger that," Perry answered. He held up the ballistic vest in his hand. "Sir, the major said the ambassador should wear this."

"Excellent idea."

McAuliffe took it, wrestled himself into it, wrapped the velcro straps around his torso. As he finished tugging on the last strap a huge explosion knocked them all off their feet, followed by two more smaller blasts in quick succession. The detonations made McAuliffe's ears ring, and he coughed and spat as the air filled with dust.

"Jesus, that was close," Katz spluttered, getting to his feet. McAuliffe steadied himself against the wall and did the same. "Time to move. We're heading for the top floor, gentlemen, using Stairwell E. Let's all get there in one piece."

Mendes led the way, with Katz and McAuliffe jogging behind. Perry and his guys had their six, and that gave McAuliffe some comfort.

As they snaked through the maze of scattered desks and chairs toward the stairwell, McAuliffe saw the extent of the damage: the light fittings that swung from the ceiling, the cracked windows, the missing scrim panels that allowed daylight to flood in. In the eastern corner of the floor, fire engulfed one of the large meeting rooms, belching black smoke across the ceiling. McAuliffe dreaded to think of the damage below and, more importantly, the casualties. They rounded a corner and Mendes stopped dead.

Ahead of them was a long corridor, the floor-to-ceiling windows overlooking the embassy grounds blown out, the walls bullet-riddled. The noise from outside was terrifying – the constant rattle of automatic weapons, the flash and bone-rattling detonations of RPGs and other munitions, the shouts and screams. McAuliffe saw the bodies lying halfway along the corridor, a man and a woman, both punctured with multiple bullet wounds. Blood was splattered across the walls. McAuliffe was glad he couldn't see their faces.

Beyond the corpses, a set of double doors. Staircase E.

"Okay, there it is," Katz said.

"Incoming!" screamed Perry.

McAuliffe caught it just as he was swamped by uniforms, a green warhead trailing smoke that spiralled towards them from a surrounding building. The detonation was close, and ceiling panels rained down on top of them. McAuliffe struggled to breathe under the weight of his protective detail, felt something hard pressing into his ribs. He fought his way out, scrambled clear of the corridor. Perry and his Marines stayed close.

"Everyone okay?" Katz asked.

McAuliffe pointed to the bodies. "That's a suicide mission, Ethan. Let's try another route."

Katz shook his head. "Can't do that. Access to Stairwell E is restricted, you know that Terry. Next entry point is the sixth floor and we got serious fires up there. The clock is ticking. This is our best shot."

"They've got it covered."

"That was a stray RPG."

McAuliffe glared at the CIA man. "I've been here before, Ethan. Baghdad, Fallujah. Guys like these will wait for hours covering a target. Now I don't mind risk – Lord knows I've taken enough of them in my time – but this is stupid. There're seven of us, a hundred feet of open corridor, and the bodies and debris are a significant obstruction. First one or two of us might make it but anyone else is going to run out of time before they light this place up. It's too risky."

"Take a look at the stairwell doors, Terry."

McAuliffe followed Katz's pointed finger. Then the penny dropped. One of the doors was hanging open, held in place by a stubborn hinge.

"When the emergency power kicks in, all safety doors in public areas switch to manual — "

"Except Staircase E," McAuliffe finished.

"Right. E, being a Special Access Zone, works the opposite way, on its own power grid. The doors seal themselves, and the only way in is with a SAP pass. Or blowing the doors."

"If they breach the building — "

"They'll be right behind us. We can't wait, Terry. We have to go, right now."

McAuliffe got to his feet, shook his legs out. "Fuck it, let's do this."

Everyone readied themselves. McAuliffe took a long look at the open corridor between them and the stairwell. The carpet was an obstacle course of broken glass, chunks of plaster and cinder block. Then there were the bodies, both sprawled across their path. They would have to be vaulted, the timing accurate. No one could risk a stumble, let alone a fall.

"Okay," McAuliffe said. "Mendes, you're on point — "

"Out of the question," Katz snapped. "I get it, you're a vet, a war hero, and that's commendable, but your safety is paramount, Terry. Our job is to get you to the roof in one piece — "

"The roof? I thought we were — "

"We're out of time, for Christ's sake. I'm going to count to three and then I'm going to sprint across that gap, and you'd better be right behind me goddammit or I'll shoot you myself." He turned to Perry. "Gunny, can you give us some cover fire?"

"Soon as you move, we'll open up."

"Mendes?"

The Marine gave a thumbs up. "Good to go."

Katz gripped McAuliffe's arm. "Ready? One, two — "

And then Katz was gone, out into the corridor, his arms and legs pumping. McAuliffe took off right behind him, making sure he lifted his knees, praying he wouldn't fall, regretting every ounce of the ballistic vest that weighed him down like an anchor. Behind him he could hear Mendes, then Perry and his Marines opened fire, the noise deafening. Up ahead he saw Katz leap over the bodies, and McAuliffe slowed for just a second as he adjusted his feet, and then he was over them, pushing for the finish line in a final sprint. He crashed through the broken door and cannoned into a waiting Katz.

McAuliffe spun around, screamed at Mendes, who reached the door just as the corridor wall behind him disintegrated in a storm of gunfire. Bullets chewed up the door to the stairwell and McAuliffe scrambled up the stairs.

"Keep moving!" Katz yelled.

"What about the Gunny, his guys — "

"No time!"

Another explosion shook the building. McAuliffe felt the shockwave through his feet, clung on to the handrail for support. The clang of falling metal echoed through the stairwell.

"Jesus Christ," Katz said, "That was *inside* the embassy."

Katz pushed past him and McAuliffe felt a hand on his back.

"Let's go," Mendes urged.

McAuliffe obeyed, following Katz as they took the stairs two at a time. The stairway was a no-frills concrete affair, narrow and stuffy with small landings every ten steps. Emergency lights lit their way, and for a minute or so all McAuliffe could hear was the scrape of their footfalls and his own breathing. It was almost a welcome relief. Then a door somewhere below them crashed open and the tension ratcheted up once more.

Everyone froze. Katz and Mendes trained their weapons down the staircase. McAuliffe waited behind them, feeling useless and naked without a firearm. Then a voice, distorted by echo, but American none the less.

"USMC! Hold your fire! I'm coming up!"

Katz shot a look at Mendes. They kept their weapons levelled, ready.

A few moments later the new arrival barrelled around the landing below and came running up the stairs. Mendes recognised him instantly.

"Jackson? What the hell are you doing here?"

McAuliffe took in the baggy combat suit and oversized helmet that seemed to wobble on the young Marine's head. He couldn't have been more than twenty years old. All McAuliffe saw was a child. And he looked terrified.

"It's gone, Mendes, all of it — "

Mendes grabbed the kid by his arm. "Hey, slow down. What's gone?"

Jackson kept looking over his shoulder as if something or someone was about to come charging up the stairs behind him.

"The lobby, the guys. It's gone. They're all dead."

McAuliffe saw that the kid was struggling to keep it together, like a sprinter in the starting blocks, his head swivelling over his shoulder, ready to bolt. He gently elbowed Mendes aside and gripped Jackson's arm.

"Look at me, son. You know who I am?"

Jackson nodded quickly. "Yes, sir."

"Good. Now take a breath and tell us what happened."

"All of us in the lobby, we were getting cut to pieces, small arms, grenades, fuckin' RPGs. Every door and gate had been blown out, then they rolled in the smoke grenades, dozens of them. Couldn't see shit. That's when the suicide bombers came in. Five or six of them maybe, no screaming or shouting, real quiet like. Next minute they were right on top of us. Boom! After that, it got real quiet. I lost my rifle, crawled over Major Vincenzo. He was dead, cut in half. Everyone was dead. Last thing I saw, the Hajis were pouring into the lobby, fanning out, real professional like. They were shooting the bodies, making sure. One of them saw me on the stairs and cut loose with an AK but I was already gone, man. I made it to the stairs, heard the gunfire up on three. I found Gunny Perry and a few others, all dead. I grabbed a weapon, saw the stairwell, made a run for it..."

Jackson's voice trailed off. McAuliffe snapped his fingers in front of Jackson's nose and once again it seemed to focus him.

"We're gonna fucking die, right here in London — "

Mendes pushed past McAuliffe and slapped Jackson

hard around the face, knocking his helmet to the floor. McAuliffe flinched and stepped back.

Mendes gripped the traumatised Marine by his chest rig and shook him. "Get your shit together, fast, Jackson. You hear me?" Mendes hit him again, harder this time, the slap echoing around the stairwell.

"Hey!" Jackson objected, his eyes narrowing.

"You getting mad?" Mendes asked. "Good, because those motherfuckers down there just killed all our guys. You want to do something about that, Jackson?" Mendes let him go, leaned in close. "You're a Marine, goddammit. Start acting like one."

Jackson said nothing, just picked his helmet up. He put it on, tightened the strap, held Mendes' gaze. Mendes jabbed him in the chest.

"Go back down to the sixth floor, keep watch. Right now that's the only way into this stairwell and you might need to buy us some time. Got that?" Jackson nodded. "Go."

Jackson charged back down the stairs and out of sight.

"Nice work," McAuliffe told Mendes.

"Let's keep moving," Katz urged. "The kid'll catch us up."

They'd made it to the tenth floor before they heard gunfire, hammering the walls of the stairwell. A few moments later feet pounded the stairs and a voice called out.

"Jackson coming up!"

The young Marine appeared a moment later, breathing hard on the landing.

"They're right behind us," he blurted. "I dropped a couple, rigged a grenade behind the door. At least we'll know when they're in the stairwell."

"Move!" Katz ordered

McAuliffe took the stairs two at a time, heart pounding, his breath coming in ragged gasps. He thought about the embassy staff, *his people,* now locked inside the emergency shelters below ground. They had food, water, enough to last for a few days. Then what? Would the situation change, control be restored? Washington would be in uproar, demand action. The Brits would deploy troops for sure, and knowing them as he did, they'd engage the enemy with unbridled ferocity. But London was a chaotic scene if Mendes' eye-witness account was anything to go by. Who knew what would happen?

By the time they reached the top floor, McAuliffe was breathing hard. As he leaned against the wall he found himself on a small, enclosed landing with a single, grey steel door set into a small alcove. The sign on the door read: *Machine Room. Authorised Personnel Only*. Katz produced his Special Access Pass from under his ballistic vest and turned to Mendes. Before he could speak a sharp detonation from below rolled over them. They heard someone scream and Jackson grinned.

"Die in agony, asshole."

"Let's get inside," Katz said.

Harsh whispers drifted up from below, the sound of fast moving feet and the rattle of equipment rising rapidly up the chamber. Katz swiped his card through the reader. A low *beep* followed, then the sound of electronic bolts disengaging. McAuliffe cringed as the sound reverberated down the stairwell. There was a shout from below. Katz yanked the door open and motioned them all inside. He pulled the heavy door closed behind him, slammed the thick bolts home. McAuliffe found himself in a small room, bare concrete walls and floor. There was another steel door set into the opposite wall.

"Will it hold?" McAuliffe asked.

"The door?" The CIA man nodded. "Four-inch thick blast-proof steel, held in place by a steel mesh frame that extends two feet into the surrounding wall, sub-surface hinges – be easier to tunnel in. Mendes, Jackson, you guys wait here. I'll take care of the ambassador."

McAuliffe followed Katz to the other door. The CIA man swiped, and the door swung inwards on pneumatic hinges.

"We've got power up here?"

"Localised, all batteries, stored energy. Very efficient. Inside, quickly."

McAuliffe did as he was told. It was dark inside, except for a couple of small red lights that glowed in the void. The door hissed closed behind them. McAuliffe felt as if his ears were about to pop.

"What are we hiding up here?" he asked Katz.

"I think you already know."

He heard the snap of a switch. Wall-mounted fittings flickered and blazed, bathing the room in bright white light.

"Holy shit," McAuliffe whispered. He took a step forward, hesitant at first, as he circled the craft with a mixture of fear and wonderment.

Ladies and gentlemen, I give you the Boeing Systems Emergency Evacuation Vehicle.

He remembered the words, and the Air Force colonel at White Sands Missile Range in New Mexico who'd delivered them. He remembered watching the test flight, the live feed from the cockpit as the EEV skimmed across dry lake beds and low, rocky hills. It had been an interesting two days, and the assembled State Department folk, including

McAuliffe, had not taken anything too seriously. An escape vehicle, fully automated, to be used only in the direst of emergencies; McAuliffe never believed he'd ever be in need of such a craft. How wrong could he be? Katz's voice interrupted his thoughts.

"Some of our embassies have them, Baghdad, Riyadh, but this is one of only three in Europe. Okay, I've got a pre-launch checklist to run through. There's a flight suit, underclothing and safety helmet in the locker over there. Lose what you're wearing and get dressed quickly."

McAuliffe did as he was told, dropping his shredded trousers, ballistic vest and filthy white shirt. He ripped open a plastic packet, pulled on the Helikon underwear set, slipped into the utility jumpsuit, strapped on the lightweight ballistic helmet. He knew the flight would be subsonic, that he would experience only low Gs, that the cockpit was pressurised, the systems fully automated. None of that made him feel any easier. He stared at the vehicle before him, tilted on its ramp towards the ceiling. It was twenty-two feet long, slate-grey in colour and made of some kind of ballistic composite. Black stars and stripes decorated the tail fin. The craft was propelled by a single jet engine, compact, quiet, hugely fuel-efficient and highly classified. *Incredibly light and virtually indestructible.* He remembered those words too. He prayed that the Air Force colonel was right.

The open cockpit hatch was made of clear Plexiglas and inside, multi-coloured displays confirmed that the vehicle was drawing power. McAuliffe flinched as a loud concussion rippled through the room.

"They're trying to blast the main door," Katz said. "Get aboard, Terry."

McAuliffe climbed into the cockpit and dropped into

the seat. The craft was surprisingly comfortable, the cockpit more spacious than he remembered, the flight panel as sophisticated as any modern fighter plane – without the flight controls. He strapped himself in, helped by Katz who was clearly familiar with the systems.

"That's your altimeter, your course heading, and the TV screen is a feed from a forward-looking thermal and low-light camera system. The compartment by your left leg contains water, rations, survival kit, but don't worry, you shouldn't need any of that." He pointed to the sat phone nestled in its mount on the panel. The display glowed green, the signal strength five by five, the battery icon fully charged. "Don't touch it. They'll call you."

When McAuliffe spoke, his own voice sounded different. He was nervous, he knew that, and he tried to shake it off, inject a little confidence. "Okay, so where can I expect to end up in this thing?"

"No clue. Somewhere safer than here, that's for sure."

McAuliffe recalled that as soon as an EEV launched anywhere in the world the DOD's SATCOM network would detect it and download target data to the craft's navigation systems. He felt the craft tremble around him as more explosions detonated outside the stairwell.

Katz was punching keys at a small terminal against the wall, running through his checklist. Then he climbed up onto the craft. "That's it, you're good to go." He leaned in and shook McAuliffe's hand.

"I feel like a fucking asshole running out like this."

"Don't sweat it. You're a target. Getting you out of here is a victory for us." He slapped his hand on the airframe. "You launch in one minute. Handholds are on either side of your seat. Good luck, Godspeed."

Katz locked the cockpit cover into place and McAuliffe

felt it seal with a quiet *thunk*. Suddenly it became quiet, the air inside the cockpit dead, just the quiet hum of electronic systems. He gave Katz a nervous thumbs up and then the CIA man was gone. In that moment, McAuliffe knew he'd never see him again.

He braced himself for – what exactly? He ran an eye over the instrumentation in front of him. Apart from the basics, he didn't have a clue what the readouts were telling him. The display on the TV monitor was just an opaque square, probably because the camera on the nose was pointed at the ceiling and —

Holy shit! The ceiling! He forgot to ask how the EEV would —

Then the craft began to vibrate and he glanced at the controls. On the upper right-hand corner of one of the displays, he noticed a small digital clock that was counting down from six, five, four... *here we go.*

Heart pounding, McAuliffe reached down and gripped the handholds by his thighs. He flinched as four sharp bangs detonated above his head and blinked as light flooded into the bay. The rooftop had been blasted away to reveal a rectangle of deep-blue sky.

The digital countdown reached zero.

The engine behind him roared.

Clouds of steam blotted out the sky. The sudden acceleration crushed him into his seat and then the craft was punching through white cloud and out into the evening sky. He grunted through gritted teeth, saw the altimeter climb to over a thousand feet, and then the craft stopped vibrating, the roar of its launch replaced by a low hum. The nose settled, then dipped, like the car at the top of a rollercoaster, and then it nosed down. McAuliffe gripped the handholds harder as the sprawl of the city came into view. Towers of smoke dotted the horizon, and then the craft descended lower, levelling off at two hundred feet, the ground passing quickly beneath the nose of the EEV. He checked the display panel. Everything was in the green, all systems nominal. He breathed a sigh of relief, then was hit by a sudden wave of guilt. He felt like a coward, the bitter shame that squeezed his throat was like nothing he'd ever experienced in his life.

As the EEV carried him to safety above a city at war, McAuliffe's thoughts turned to the people he'd left behind and prayed that somehow they'd make it out okay.

For the Jihadi sleeper teams, the crucial targets were the military ones.

They had trained hard, back in the Caliphate, and on return to their host countries had met frequently, and always in secret. They formed small teams, acquired weapons and equipment, planned their attacks, welcomed those individuals from the Martyr Brigades, the men and women who had only one job: destroy their targets at the cost of their own lives.

Yet if anything could slow the invasion, it would be the combined forces of the European armies. Fortunately, with the Cold War resigned to the history books and the European Union long descended into a political quagmire of self-interest and in-fighting, the bulwark of a once mighty NATO that stood in defence of Europe was no more. The Americans had packed up and gone home, no longer willing to sacrifice the lives of US servicemen and women in defence of a continent that often held their country in contempt. All that remained were a small group of administrative and advisory staff, less than a hundred personnel, all stationed at EUFOR, the European Forces Headquarters in Brussels, Belgium.

Like the Americans, the British presence in Europe had also dwindled over the years. Now they maintained just a single site in Germany, a light-armoured garrison in Paderborn forming part of the EU's High Readiness Joint Task Force. The British troops were an armoured infantry unit, comprising five hundred men, a dozen Warrior fighting vehicles, infantry and various support elements. Although a small contingent, the British troops were considered to be a significant threat. They had to be hit hard. And just before 7 pm local time, they were.

The lead truck in a convoy of four rolled along the Staumuehler Strasse towards Normandy Barracks at 6:58 pm. Surrounded by stone walls twelve feet high and topped with razor wire, the camp consisted of accommodation blocks, administration buildings, equipment stores, a petrol, oil and diesel compound, garage and maintenance sheds, and various other buildings. There were four access gates, three of which were unmanned but heavily secured. The main gate was on the Staumuehler Strasse itself, through which all vehicular and pedestrian traffic passed. At 7 pm on a warm summer evening, traffic was light.

The lead truck, a thirty-tonne flatbed covered with sheeted crates, rumbled slowly along the quiet, tree-lined street and turned into the camp. The driver was waved to a halt in front of a heavy red and white security gate manned by two bored British soldiers. Four hundred yards away along the Staumuehler Strasse, three similar trucks waited, their engines idling.

At the main gate, one of the guards climbed up onto the running board and quizzed the driver whilst his compatriot walked along the side of the flatbed, tugging in vain at the tarpaulin. The driver handed over a mess of paperwork, all in German but clearly stamped with the legend *Normandy Barracks*. The soldier looked at the crumpled mess and decided he didn't get paid enough to sort it all out. That privilege would fall on the shoulders of the duty NCO in the main guardhouse. The soldier ordered the barrier raised and directed the driver to pull into the parking bay just inside the gate. He walked across to the guardroom, papers in hand, thinking he might enjoy watching the duty corporal bemoan his luck. After all, the arrogant prick was always banging on about how much more he got paid than a lowly private. *And* he didn't speak German. Bonus.

Language skills were the last thought ever to pass through the young soldier's mind as the driver of the flatbed detonated the two-thousand-pound bomb lashed to the back of the truck. The white-hot flash and ear-shattering detonation disintegrated the guardroom, obliterated the camp gates and a hundred yards of the perimeter wall, and shattered every window for six hundred yards. Four miles away, in the centre of town, people stopped in the street and looked up at the sky.

On the Staumuehler Strasse, the other three trucks gunned their engines and headed for the breach in the camp's defences. One by one, they rumbled into the barracks, swerving around the large crater and bouncing over the still-smoking rubble strewn across the road. Soldiers from across the camp came running towards the scene of the blast. Now, they scattered for their lives as the trucks thundered towards them, crushing dozens beneath their wheels.

Each driver was assigned a target. The first truck left the road and bounced over grassy verges towards the accommodation blocks, located side by side in neat, Germanic lines. The truck aimed for the area between the first of two, three-storey buildings, most of which would be populated with British troops, according to his intelligence. Seconds later the driver detonated his device. The resulting explosion levelled both buildings in a devastating wave of heat and pressure. Over a hundred personnel died instantly.

The two remaining trucks headed for their own targets, the main fuel store and the sheds that housed the armoured vehicles. The fuel store was the first to go, the explosion sending a huge fireball hundreds of feet into the air and splashing burning fuel over a wide area.

The driver of the last truck was ecstatic and screamed a victorious battle cry as he gunned his vehicle into the rusting metal sheds and exploded it, completely destroying four Warriors and severely damaging several others.

In the wake of the devastation – and cloaked by a blanket of secondary explosions, fire and smoke – fifty Jihadi fighters charged into the camp, cutting down every living thing they could see with automatic weapons and grenades. A few British soldiers managed to get into the armoury and grab weapons but it was a futile gesture. Outgunned and taken completely by surprise, the survivors armed up and fled the camp in small groups, disappearing into the surrounding streets.

To all intents and purposes, British forces on the European mainland were out of the fight.

THREE THOUSAND MILES TO THE SOUTH-EAST, DEEP beneath the Jabal Sawda mountains, the Grand Mufti Mohammed Wazir gazed at the huge battlefield display screen that covered a whole wall of the busy command centre. He said nothing, nor gave any indication of his inner emotions. Around him, scores of operators sat at their communications consoles and processed real-time battle-field information from T-BIS, the Chinese-built Theatre-wide Battlefield Information System.

T-BIS was driven by an electronic thirst for informa-tion. From whole army groups down to squad-level units, T-BIS was a fully integrated, digital GPS monitoring system that could pinpoint every element of the Islamic State's armed forces at any given time. Using credit-card-sized digital transponders installed on a wide variety of men and material, the resulting signals could be relayed via a multi-tude of stations, from airborne elements to static ground and mobile transmitters. It provided its controllers with a visual real-time map of where its planes were in the sky, its naval forces at sea, its mechanised elements and its personnel – all the way down to squad level.

Right now, mobile T-BIS units were pushing into Europe right behind the forward elements, relaying their information back to the command centre via designated MILSPEC aircraft flying high over the Mediterranean or via the Caliphate's main relay stations dotted along the North African coastline. In air-conditioned caverns deep under the Jabal Sawda, the central processing server clus-ters translated the billions of bytes of information it received into graphical images and uploaded them onto the giant screen while the one hundred and seventy-two operators – divided into Airforce, Army and Naval groups – collated that information and fed it to the battlefield commanders and the theatre Generals who reported to the Grand Mufti Wazir himself.

Wazir watched in silence as the campaign played out across the huge screen above him. The display was currently projecting a digital relief map of western Europe, overlaid with hundreds of blue icons indicating IS and Turkish military units. Those icons had now crossed the European frontier and were beginning to spread out across the continent. To the north, red icons representing Russian forces streamed into Poland and were advancing westwards. The defending European forces were symbolised by purple icons. Since the start of hostilities, over half had disappeared from the display.

A military aide approached Wazir, a computer printout in his hand. He stopped a few feet short and coughed politely. Wazir turned.

"Yes, Colonel Asiri?"

"Your Eminence, if it pleases you I would like to update you on our present situation."

Wazir turned away from the display and beckoned Asiri to follow. "My quarters."

The Colonel trailed at a respectful distance as Wazir made his way up a steel staircase towards the mezzanine-level gantry. The Cleric's private suite was well-appointed, decorated with comfortable furniture and deep rugs on the stone floor. A smaller T-BIS screen mounted on the far wall glowed brightly in the dimness of the cavern. Wazir eased himself into a straight-backed chair and pointed to the display.

"Your report, Colonel."

The intelligence officer cleared his throat. "Early indications suggest that our surprise attacks have been a success, your eminence. Far better than we'd hoped."

"Go on."

"The cruise missile attacks were over ninety percent successful, and a significant amount of enemy hardware and infrastructure has been completely destroyed. Initial reports also indicate that the sleeper teams have been extremely effective in neutralising, disabling or disrupting their targets. Civil, administrative and police forces across Europe are in significant disarray.'

Asiri flicked through the printout, glancing at Wazir in order to determine his mood, but the older man remained impassive, sitting in silence as he absorbed the details. The Colonel pressed on.

"Forward Air Controllers have cleared the skies in preparation for the airborne assault. Advance units have already landed in both Spain and southern France without any serious opposition, and in northern Europe, Russian forces are pushing towards the German frontier. Opposition is light and disorganised across the whole theatre."

Wazir leaned forward in his chair. "And what of the civilian populations? Our people?"

"Community leaders across Europe have responded as planned, Your Eminence. Every assistance has been given to the Jihadi teams and preparations made for the arrival of our main forces. Infidel police and military units are being attacked where possible and roadblocks put into place as directed. Intelligence suggests that the Infidels are staying in their homes or remain trapped in their workplaces. Casualties are considerable of course, and the emergency services have collapsed under the pressure. Law and order are non-existent."

Wazir smiled and said, "Europe holds its breath. The Infidels will ask, *what is coming next?* They will cower in their homes, frightened, confused. As night falls that fear will increase. They will have no electricity, no communications. The police will not come, their governments silent and powerless, unable to hear their cries for help. Psychologically, this is a crucial time for our forces. But there will be others, mostly young, who will venture out onto the streets. They will be inquisitive, cautious. Apprehensive, yes, but not yet frightened. They will have seen the chaos and smelled opportunity. They will form groups and arm themselves. They will loot and cause destruction and they will react violently when confronted with others of their kind. When they meet our forces, they will resist."

"Indeed," Asiri nodded. "Violent uprisings have already occurred across many European cities. Some suburbs of Paris and London are already in flames, with much of that violence not of our making. These pockets of potential resistance will be eliminated quickly enough as the main spearhead forces begin to seize control, aided and abetted by the sleeper teams and the militia units formed by our own people." Wazir rose from his chair and wandered over to the display on the wall, staring intently at the glowing icons on the digital map.

Asiri watched carefully. It was always so difficult to judge the man's mood, but he would surely appreciate that the campaign was proceeding better than they could have hoped for. Or maybe not. Wazir often measured things differently. Fundamentally, he was opposed to bloodshed. He had often lectured that violence as a tool for bloody revenge had achieved nothing in the Middle East and he had been proved right. His own rise to power had been carefully planned and his reputation of persuasion and coercion rather than violence and the spilling of blood had increased his standing amongst opponents and political rivals. Of course, there were also times when violence had been inevitable: such was their culture.

"And what of the British?" Wazir asked. "Our Brothers and Sisters have waited patiently for this day. How goes the operation there?"

The Colonel scanned his printout. "Invasion forces are

ashore and are beginning to push out from their marshalling areas. Military transports carrying air assault forces have crossed the English Channel and are heading for their designated target airports and drop zones. The story in Britain is much the same as in the rest of Europe, Your Eminence. Victory is almost certainly assured."

Wazir turned, and for the first time since Asiri had been assigned to his command team, the older man smiled.

"Your report has been most informative, Colonel. Keep me abreast of any significant developments."

"As you wish."

Asiri bowed politely and hurried from the room.

EASTERN ATLANTIC

Twenty-two miles due west off the coast of Portugal, the *USS New Jersey* cruised through the gentle swell of an unusually calm Atlantic Ocean, its sleek grey-blue hull almost lost against the darkening sky as it silently tracked the line of merchant ships five miles ahead of them.

The two hundred and forty-foot long ship represented the new generation of Windward class stealth surface craft that had been developed by the US Navy and the *New Jersey* was at the cutting edge of that technology. Essentially a huge trimaran, the ship was likened to a B-2 stealth bomber on water, her bridge situated at the very front of the ship, its rounded superstructure jutting out over the water like the nose of an aircraft. From its sides, two large 'wings' dipped towards the surface of the sea and gave the *New Jersey* its stability and buoyancy. There wasn't a single right-angle to her design, nothing that could give a potential enemy a radar return of any significance until the ship was well within missile range.

Like her sister ship the *USS California,* the *New Jersey*

was small, weighing in at just over twenty-two thousand tonnes, and very stealthy. She was equipped with the Navy's latest variant of the Aegis weapons system, including RIM missiles and a Phalanx CIWS, but her deadliest weapon was her speed. Powered by eight ultra-quiet water-jet engines clustered at the stern and on her wings, a fully-loaded *New Jersey* was capable of speeds of up to seventy-two knots on light to moderate swells. In heavy seas, she was reduced to around thirty-five, but she was still the fastest naval surface craft in the world – and classified Top Secret.

The crew was handpicked, the best at what they did, and all were cleared for *New Jersey's* wide range of classified missions. The only downside, according to her crew, was the fact that the *New Jersey* had a single open deck, a narrow, thirty-foot long covered gantry at the rear of the ship above the centre hull. It's why they called her the *Bat Ship*.

Captain Frank Schelling knew of *New Jersey's* moniker and thought it suited her pretty well. Wherever possible they avoided major shipping lanes during daylight hours, utilising the vast solitude of the Atlantic Ocean until darkness descended. Then she lived up to her moniker, flitting between vessels in crowded shipping lanes, trailing foreign naval vessels undetected, sometimes in their very wake, tracking multiple military targets unseen during allied exercises. And when people did see her up close and personal, it was usually a lone sailing vessel somewhere far out in the emptiness, a rare glimpse of the strange, bird-like ship that seemed to glide across the surface of the water. The rumours, the shaky YouTube videos, only added to her mystery. And whenever *New Jersey* returned to her home port at Kitsap, Maine, they did so at night, the Navy unwilling to advertise their stealth flagships to anyone but cleared naval personnel and those who worked inside the restricted, specialised pen in which *New Jersey* was maintained and resupplied. Schelling was more than proud to be her master and commander.

Right now, that pride had been replaced by a growing interest in other traffic that was currently riding the light Atlantic swell. Thirty minutes earlier, as Schelling sat in the captain's chair, his Combat Management System alerted him to an extended line of twelve civilian merchantmen tooling past Cabo de Sao Vicente, the point where ships leaving the Mediterranean turned north into the busy shipping lanes towards the Bay of Biscay and the ports of northern Europe. Schelling's interest had been piqued when the convoy had accelerated to nearly eighteen knots, which was mighty unusual for a merchant vessel, let alone a convoy of them.

The *New Jersey* had closed under cover of the gathering darkness to within five miles of the ships, and now Schelling watched twelve blips, all evenly spaced and running at full speed, track slowly across the CMS's multi-target radar display. He ordered his LongBow low-light thermal imaging camera system to track the lead ship. He glanced up at the flat-panel display screen above his chair. The target ship, like the others, was observing some kind of black-out drill which again was odd for a merchantman. One minute their running lights were on, next minute they were —

Shit!

Schelling's warning panel blinked red and an accompanying buzzer sounded around the bridge. One of the merchantmen had just lit off an air-search radar, making three quick sweeps of the sky before shutting down again. Over the comms net, CIC reported the radar signature to be a military set, high power. *What the hell were merchies doing with military-spec radar sets?* wondered Schelling. No sooner had the thought crossed his mind when his comms officer alerted him to an incoming *Eyes Only* flash-traffic message. Schelling took it, read it.

"Goddam," he breathed quietly. Then he strapped himself into the captain's seat. That raised every eyebrow on the bridge. "Mister Andrews, send the tracking data to Task Force Command and break us off from the merchies. Secure the ship for a high-speed run to this position."

He handed the message slip to his Executive Officer who passed it on to the navigation team. The coordinates were quickly punched into the CMS and Schelling received a green confirmation light on his own display.

"Co-ordinates locked and confirmed, sir." Andrews grabbed his handset and dialled into the ship's PA system. "Bridge to crew, Bridge to crew, now hear this. All hands secure for high-speed run."

Within two minutes the ship was readied, the crew strapped in for the run. All lights were green across the board and that pleased Schelling greatly. The periodic drilling of his crew was certainly showing results; nearly seven seconds better than their previous attempt. Except this time it wasn't a drill.

"Mister Andrews, bring us about to course zero-one-zero degrees. Make your speed sixty knots. Keep us out of the shipping lanes but let's get to our destination as quickly as possible."

"Aye aye, sir."

Andrews repeated the order to the two pilots in front of

him and immediately Schelling felt the ship change course and begin to gently vibrate as it accelerated across the waves. The captain checked his display. Already they were approaching thirty knots. Even after fifteen months as her commander, Schelling was still thrilled by the power of the water-jet engines and the speed at which the sea disappeared below the nose of the ship.

"Nav, Status."

"Eight – correction, *nine* merchant vessels dead ahead, all headed due north. Nearest target is twelve miles and closing. We'll pass two clicks off her starboard bow. That'll take us out of the major shipping lanes in approximately thirty-six minutes. There's a fishing fleet north of us, seventy-five miles off Cabo De Sines. Target count is twenty-two vessels, scattered configuration. Recommend a two-degree course change to port to clear their nets in zero-two minutes."

"Make it so."

Andrews beeped Schelling on his secure headset. Although only six feet away, he was safely strapped into his own seat. It would be foolish and not a little dangerous to try and move around while the ship rocketed across the wave tops at fifty-eight point seven knots.

"Question," Andrews asked quietly.

"Let me guess...*where are we going?*"

"Aye, sir."

"We'll get an update when we arrive on station. All I know is that there'll be a man in the water when we get there. Or shortly afterwards."

"A rescue mission?"

"Not officially. We are not to broadcast a public mayday and we're to avoid all contact with other vessels, friendly or otherwise."

"So, it's an exercise."

"No." Schelling lowered his voice to just above a whisper. "We've just been authorised to use deadly force. We're officially at DEFCON Three and I have absolutely no clue why."

In the dim red glow of the bridge, Andrews paled.

CENTRAL LONDON
ST JAMES' PARK

Chris Hunt nursed his second cup of tea, comforted by the fact that he was, momentarily at least, out of danger.

He was seated on a large sofa in a darkened drawing room, lit only by a few candles and the warm glow of an open fire. Facing him across a coffee table, the white-haired old man who'd given him sanctuary was pouring boiling water into a mug, fussing with the brew until he appeared satisfied. Then he leaned back in his armchair and sipped the beverage quietly, a look of satisfaction on his lined face.

Yet Stewart Murray's unruffled manner was already getting under Chris' skin. From the moment he'd pushed past the old codger, desperately searching for another way out, Murray's initial assurances had done nothing to quell his panic. He'd ducked from room to room, looking for an escape route, a hiding place, expecting to hear angry shouts outside, pounding on the front door, the crack of gunfire. Instead, what he heard was Murray bolting the door behind him, his assurances that he hadn't been spotted, that they were both perfectly safe as long as they remained calm

102

and quiet, and stayed away from the windows. After a few minutes, Chris had taken a breath and realised that the old man was right.

He was safe. For now.

Murray had invited him into the gloomy drawing room, thrust a stiff scotch in his hand, and ordered him to sit. Chris did as instructed, and for a long time they'd sat in silence, listening to the sounds of gunfire, feeling the tremor of large explosions as they shook the ground beneath their feet. As the evening wore on, the sounds of battle lessened, the nearby fighting all but stopped. Or moved on. Chris would settle for either.

He leaned back into the sofa, suddenly exhausted. The adrenaline that had kept him going over the last few hours had taken its toll. He stared at the ceiling and let out a long, deep breath.

"Feeling better?" Murray asked.

Chris dropped his chin. "I'm fine." Murray was smiling, sipping his tea. Chris couldn't help himself. "Do you realise what's going on out there? It's a terror attack, a massive one. Thousands of people are dead, lying all over the streets — " He felt the tremor in his throat and cleared it quickly.

"Best we stay here then," Murray said, thin lips fixed in a smile. "Why don't you drink your tea? You'll feel better."

"*Drink tea?* Jesus," Chris snorted, "maybe I should keep a stiff upper lip as well, keep calm and carry on, all that wartime shit."

"Getting upset isn't going to help."

"I'm not upset." *I'm fucking terrified, you silly old bastard,* Chris didn't say. But he wanted to. How did Murray stay so calm? It was age, he decided. Murray was what, late seventies? In the grand scheme of things, his time was running out, the clock ticking faster with each passing year. Apparently, death held little fear for the elderly. Chris, on the other hand, had everything to live for.

"I've been in this type of situation before," said Murray. "We keep our heads down, keep out of sight, we should be fine. I'm quite well stocked on the essentials, and I have a camping stove with plenty of gas. Hopefully, the situation will have resolved itself long before we run out of supplies."

"The situation?" Chris echoed. "Maybe you should go for a stroll around the block, see what's going on out there."

"No thanks, quite comfortable here," Murray chuckled.

"You think this is a joke? Are you stupid?" Chris saw Murray's smile slip. "That's right, not so funny when you think about it."

Murray put down his tea, swung one leg over the other and leaned back in his chair. "You're angry because you're frightened. I understand that. I'm frightened too, but I'm not going to let it control me. Fear breeds panic, and panic can lead to poor decision making. We're comfortable here, below ground, sheltered from the violence. We have an opportunity to take stock, consider our options, wait for news, official word, something. I'm smiling, not because I'm amused or unaware of the horrors that are taking place outside my door; I'm smiling because it's preferable to the alternative, one that's written all over your face, Inspector Hunt."

Murray peered over his heavy-rimmed spectacles.

"I see panic, fear and anger. I see a man who has been through a great deal in a short space of time, and I'm trying to offer that man a sliver of normality, an opportunity to take a breath, ground his feet, gather his strength – both physical and emotional. I'm offering sanctuary, Inspector Hunt. I hope you can see that."

"It's Chief Inspector."

Murray reached for a tobacco pouch on the table and began rolling a thin cigarette. A deep rumble rattled the montage of framed photographs on the wall behind him.

Chris swallowed involuntarily. "Bloody hell, that was a big one."

"Not an explosion," Murray speculated, his head cocked to one side. "More like a building collapse."

Chris got to his feet, drawn to the faded gallery of images behind Murray. It was the usual, depressing display of traditionalist, white middle-class conservatism; several shots of a presumably dead wife, children, grandchildren. Generic, predictable. Boring. Then he saw a photograph of a much younger Murray, posing in front of a large pile of rubble, smiling for the camera as soldiers wearing blue helmets loitered by an armoured personnel carrier behind him.

"Where was that taken?"

He heard the creak of leather as Murray swivelled in his seat. "That one? Aleppo. In Syria."

"I know where Aleppo is," Chris told him. "What were you doing over there?"

"I used to work for Save the Children, as a logistics coordinator. Did a lot of work in the Middle East for them, until the Caliphate swept across the region and ordered us out. Those are Brazilian peacekeeping troops." Murray paused for a moment, lighting his cigarette with a zippo and exhaling a thin stream of blue smoke. "So you see, I have some experience with living under siege, Chief Inspector — "

"It's Chris."

"Chris," Murray repeated. "I have a son called Chr — "

"Do you mind?" Chris tutted, swatting the air. "I really don't like cigarette smoke."

Murray looked suitably embarrassed. "Yes, selfish of me. Didn't think to ask, circumstances being what they are." He stubbed it out in a glass ashtray.

Chris sat down again, helped himself to a generous tumbler of scotch from the bottle on the table. Murray twisted the cap back on and set the bottle down by his chair.

Chris felt the warmth of the alcohol soothing his frayed nerves. "I called you stupid earlier. I apologise."

Murray held up his hand. "Please, there's no need. I understand." He drained his mug and set it down on the coffee table. "Where have you come from? What station, I mean?"

Chris hesitated. His instincts for avoiding potentially difficult questions had been carefully honed over the years. The truth was he'd abandoned his post, left his team deep underground, concerned only for his personal safety. And he'd survived, that was the important thing, the only other witness to his escape, Mark Meloy, now a charred lump lying at the bottom of that distant stairwell. The others, the civilians in the office, well, they might be dead too by now. He could write his own story, control the narrative. He'd lose a few rounds from the Glock; there were enough bodies out on the street for Chris to claim one or two as his own. He wouldn't be the only hero to emerge from this crisis but he'd make damn sure that he'd be up on the podium with the rest of them, having a medal pinned to his uniform, smiling and shaking hands for the photographer. If and when this crisis blew over.

"I work over on Victoria Street," Chris told him.

"I'm not aware of any station there."

"It's an operational building. You wouldn't know about it."

"What do you do there?"

"I head up the Special Operations Room," Chris said, then instantly regretted it. The old man didn't need to know that, but he'd just blabbed it out.

Murray nodded. "Yes, I've heard of the place. Saw it on the news once, very high-tech, lots of CCTV and computers. You work there?"

"I'm in charge."

"What are you doing here? I mean, what were you doing out on the street?"

Chris got to his feet. "Can I use your toilet?"

Murray pointed. "Turn right, second on the left. If it's just a pee, don't flush. Water conservation and all that. Until we know."

Chris locked the door behind him. He lowered the lid, sat on the toilet and fumed. He had to get his story straight. A couple of questions from a doddery old man and already he'd given away far too much information. He had to construct a coherent, plausible story as to why the head of the SOR was seen skulking beneath a car four streets away from where he should've been.

He leaned forward, massaged his face. He thought about Anton then, realised he hadn't thought about him for some time. He'd be okay, Chris was sure of that. Anton was practical, level-headed, despite being a fussy creative type. Often it was Anton who took charge at home, and Chris was happy to let him do it because he knew deep down that he wasn't a natural leader himself.

He was well aware that the reason for his rapid rise up the police ranks had much to do with him being gay. He'd pressed that advantage too, knowing that the system would favour him over heterosexual candidates, that any rejection would be met with an appeal, a subtle threat of anti-discriminatory action and bad press. Most of his gay colleagues had applied the tactic successfully throughout their own careers, often mirroring the actions of their more militant ethnic minority colleagues who screamed racism at every opportunity in order to bend the system to their will. And by and large, it had worked. He often joked with Anton and their friends about it and speculated how far Anton would've risen up the ranks being both gay *and* black. How they'd all laughed at that one.

But none of that helped now. And another, darker train of thought was beginning to form in Chris' mind. He was only too aware of what happened to gay men behind the 'Iron Veil' of the Caliphate: the rumours of mass arrests, beatings, the unforgiving Sharia courts, the grisly executions. Gay communities all over Europe would often march freely through their own capitals, protesting every injustice they could think of to further their own cause, to tear down archaic institutions and overturn traditions in order to paint the world pink. But Chris knew they all stayed silent in the face of certain other uncomfortable truths, the closure of gay bars and clubs in 'sensitive' areas, the ever-increasing assaults on gay men across Europe by so-called Sharia patrols, the condemnation and open hostility of Islamic community leaders. Like most of his community, and much of the Establishment, Chris didn't dare challenge Muslims on their attitudes to homosexuality. Instead, he'd always turned a blind eye and focused on easier targets instead.

Now there were armed men, *Muslim men,* roaming the streets outside. Chris felt uncomfortable even thinking in such terms. He'd been conditioned to never question the beauty of Islam, the peace-loving Muslim community, yet his eyes were telling him something else. Whatever the reality, he had to wait it out until the dust settled and order was restored. So, he would use that time to concoct a cover story, sticking as close to the truth as possible but embellishing it, not too much, but enough to earn him another promotion. That should be his focus now. He stood up and flushed the loo.

He found Murray in the kitchen, washing up. "I'll make up the spare bed for you, Chris. It'll be getting dark soon and that's always dangerous in situations like this. The front and back doors are very secure and the windows are all grilled, this being a basement flat. We'll keep the curtains closed, the candlelight to a minimum. Thing's will look different in the morning I'm sure."

"What about your neighbours?"

"The apartment above us is actually an office, a recruitment agency. There's another apartment on the top floor but I rarely see the owners." Murray pointed to Chris' coat. "The pistol you're carrying. Is it safe?"

"Of course," snapped Chris. He yanked it out, grabbed a handful of kitchen roll and began wiping the blood off it.

"Who did it belong to?"

"I took it from — " *Shit, he'd done it again.* "A dead colleague. I needed it, for self-defence."

"Of course. Harsh words and a notebook aren't going to cut it out there," Murray smiled, "though I'd rather it was out of sight. If someone does come in, well, it could change things."

Chris held the pistol by his leg. "Where d'you want me to sleep? I'll leave it in there."

Murray wiped his hands on a tea towel. "Let me show you."

Chris followed him along the dark corridor, guided by Murray's flickering tea light. The spare bedroom was large and comfortably furnished, Chris noted. A brass posted bed, a dark wood dresser, a thick red rug on the floor. He peeked through the heavy curtains. The garden beyond was quite large, lawned and bordered with flowers, leading down to a high brick wall. Birdcage Walk lay behind the wall, St James' Park beyond that. There were no lights to be seen, and the darkening sky was lit by the odd flash. It felt like things were quietening down and that made Chris feel a little less anxious. He closed the curtain, opened one of the drawers in the dresser. He held the Glock up. "I'll leave it in here, okay?"

"Thank you," Murray nodded. Suddenly his face lit up. "Ah! There it is!"

Chris watched him pluck a small radio from behind a photograph on the bedside table.

"I tried the TV but that was dead. Knew I had a battery radio somewhere."

He sat on the bed and fiddled with the volume, the dials. It was an old-fashioned piece of kit, just a small plastic box with an extendable aerial. In the flickering glow of candlelight, Chris heard the quiet hiss of static.

"I'll try the FM band first," Murray said.

Chris leaned in closer, his ear straining to pick up any sound other than static. Where had all the stations gone? True, many of the local broadcasters transmitted from London and therefore may be incapacitated by the power cuts, but there were others, national stations, that trans-mitted from a variety of places around the country. Surely they were still up and working? Or were these events happening all over the —

"...Citizens of Britain..."

"That's it," Chris said. "Go back! Quickly!" Murray fumbled. Chris snatched it from his hands. "Give it here." He dialled it back with his thumb. The radio hissed and then a hard-edged voice filled the room:

"...is an emergency broadcast. There is a civil emergency in progress and martial law has been declared. Stay in your homes and remain calm. Failure to adhere to this message will result in immediate arrest. Deadly force has been authorised in the event of civil unrest. I repeat, stay in your homes —"

The broadcast finished a few moments later. There was a brief interlude of music and then the message repeated. Chris listened to it several times before Murray prised it from his hands and clicked it off.

"Best to save the batteries."

It was a moment before Chris could speak.

"Tell me this is one almighty fucking prank," he whispered. His anxiety was bubbling over again. He felt sick.

"I fear not," Murray said, the radio cradled in his lap like a treasured heirloom.

"What the hell are we going to do?" he asked the old man. He'd relinquished any attempt at authority. It was clear Murray was the calmer of them both, that Chris was the one with the high-pitched voice bordering on panic.

"We stay put, we watch and we wait. The sun will be up in a few hours. I suggest we get some rest, see what happens. I'll wake you at dawn. Try and get some sleep."

The door closed behind him. Chris sat on the bed, his mind reeling, his brain struggling to compute what he'd seen and heard in the last few hours. *Martial law? Deadly force? What the fuck was going on?* He lay back on the bed and stared up at the ceiling. Another distant explosion rumbled through the building. Behind the curtain the window rattled, as if there was someone there, determined to get in.

Chris whined and rolled over, burying himself beneath the thick duvet.

ATLANTIC OCEAN

"Contact! Transponder bearing zero-four-four degrees, range one-seven-five miles and closing, altitude forty-two hundred feet. Transponder ident is alpha seven-one-one. That's our bird, sir."

"Roger that. All engines stop," acknowledged Schelling. "XO, launch the rescue party and get them to circle the ship a thousand yards out. This thing could land just about anywhere."

"Aye aye, sir."

In the dimly-lit cargo belly of the ship, a water-tight hatch powered back on silent servo-motors to reveal the wave tops twenty feet below. Suspended above the open hatch in a rigid inflatable launch, six crewmen were dressed in survival suits, two of them SAR rescue swimmers. On the chief's signal, the boat was lowered down onto the water. As its twin propellers bit into the waves, the launch accelerated from under the hull and away from the ship. On the bridge, Schelling registered the new blip on his sonar screen.

"Launch is in the water, sir."

As the minutes ticked by, Schelling pondered the new

orders he'd received since arriving on station twenty-seven minutes ago. He'd briefed his officers in the wardroom and made a general crew announcement over the ship's PA. He removed the message slip from his breast pocket and read it again:

*** FLASH MESSAGE ***

   PRIORITY ONE: USS NEW JERSEY TO HOLD STATION AT -6.56 49.85. — AWAIT IMMINENT ARRIVAL OF AIRBORNE EVAC CRAFT — RECOVER VIP PASSENGER AND SCUTTLE CRAFT — MAKE ALL POSSIBLE SPEED TO JOINT EXPEDITIONARY BASE, LITTLE CREEK, VIRGINIA — ALL NON-US CONTACTS TO BE CONSIDERED UNFRIENDLY — CONFIRM SAFE AIR COVER AT SEVEN HUNDRED MILES OFF EASTERN SEABOARD — OUTLYING SURFACE PICKETS AT FOUR HUNDRED MILES. ALERT STATUS DEFCON THREE BY ORDER CINCLANT -

   *** MESSAGE ENDS ***

Schelling was both intrigued and a little concerned. *An airborne evac craft?* He'd never heard of such a thing but presumed it was something like the pod built into Air Force One. Where was it coming from? Who was inside? Whatever the details, a forced ditch at sea was a dangerous operation, to say the least. Then there was the small matter of DEFCON Three. That was virtually a shooting war, but with whom? Right now he had more questions than answers.

"What have we got, XO?"

"Target is twenty-nine clicks out, heading zero-one-four degrees, three thousand feet and descending. Estimate splash down in three and a half minutes, eight hundred yards off our port bow. Nearest surface traffic is eighty-three miles south-southwest headed towards the English Channel. Nothing close, sir."

"All ahead slow," Schelling ordered. He grabbed a pair of binoculars and went forward to the wide, sloping bridge windows. He scanned the shifting waters, the dark horizon. Behind him the bridge was silent. Andrews joined him with his own binoculars and began sweeping the ocean.

"Bridge, SRO, target is one mile and closing," radar reported over the PA. "Heading is constant, airspeed and altitude are falling. Splashdown in thirty seconds, five hundred yards off the port bow."

"Bring us around, XO. Alert the SAR team."

As the boat drifted to port, Schelling spotted it skimming low over the surface of the sea. It looked like a small fighter jet, with a pair of stubby wings and a tail fin, and as he watched, its nose dipped towards the waves. Buoyancy aids suddenly exploded around the fuselage and the drone skipped across the water, slowing quickly to a stop in a surge of white foam. Emergency lights began pulsing around the craft and Schelling was pleased to see that the rescue launch was almost there. After the passenger was transferred, Schelling watched a crewman toss a couple of grenades into the cockpit. As the boat sped away, the grenades detonated with a bright flash that lit up the surface of the sea. In a minute or so the craft was engulfed in flames and slipped beneath the waves. Ten minutes later, after a visit to the ship's doctor, the VIP was shown into Schelling's quarters...

"Captain Frank Schelling, United States Navy. Welcome aboard the *New Jersey,* sir."

McAuliffe glanced at himself in the mirror as he shook the captain's hand. The last time he did that was in London, a lifetime ago. The guy in the mirror was a stranger, with wild hair and bloodshot eyes.

"Sit down, please."

Schelling offered him the couch and McAuliffe dropped into it. "You got a drink?" The captain nodded, poured a couple of glasses of bourbon and handed one over. McAuliffe downed his in two quick swallows. Schelling refilled it and McAuliffe took a more measured sip this time, wiping the back of his hand across his mouth.

"My name is Terry McAuliffe, United States Ambassador to Great Britain."

Schelling stared at him for several moments, and then he said, "This is getting stranger by the minute."

"Do you know what's happening, captain?"

Schelling shrugged. "All I know is the order to come rescue you. Plus, the small matter of DEFCON Three."

"Jesus," McAuliffe whispered. He took another slug of booze and set the glass back on the table between them. "Okay, so let me tell you how I got here. A few hours ago, the embassy in London was attacked. Wait, that's not correct. It was *assaulted.*"

He saw Schelling frown.

"Excuse me, sir?"

"Let me explain."

And McAuliffe did, spending the next fifteen minutes describing the attack and his hair-raising, shameful escape from London. "I need to know what happened to my people," he finished. "I need to speak to Washington."

Schelling pondered the request, excused himself. A few minutes later McAuliffe could feel the ship begin to move.

Outside the captain's window, the sky was black. When Schelling returned he had an update for McAuliffe.

"I've spoken to CINCLANT, sir. My orders are to get you home asap. I'll have you escorted to your quarters. There's a shower in there and I'll have a crewman bring you some fresh clothes and some food. I'd like to get the doc to take another look at you too."

"I'm fine."

"It's not a request."

McAuliffe set his cup down, stood slowly, his aching limbs resisting the effort.

"Okay, but I have a request of my own."

"What is it?"

"If you have a spare computer I'd like to file a preliminary report. A lot of good men died so I can be here now. I need to record as much detail as possible while it's still fresh in my mind."

Schelling nodded. "I'll arrange it. Follow me, please."

Outside in the gangway, a crewman waited to escort him. They'd only taken a few paces when McAuliffe said, "This is one of those stealth ships, isn't it?"

"That's correct," Schelling confirmed.

"Are these things as fast as they say?"

Schelling nodded. "You're about to find out."

THE NEW DAY WAS STILL A PALE-YELLOW BAND ON THE far horizon.

In the pre-dawn gloom, the *New Jersey* pitched and rolled in heavy seas beneath a steel grey sky, nine nautical miles short of the Mid-Atlantic Shelf.

On the bridge, Frank Schelling watched through binoculars as a Seahawk helicopter approached his ship from the deck of the USS *Arizona*, just over a mile away across the dark waters. The *New Jersey* had made a record-breaking overnight run, but the Atlantic swells were becoming increasingly heavy and Schelling was glad to give his ship a breather. From here on in naval aviation would finish the job.

"Morning, captain."

Schelling turned, saw McAuliffe approaching, escorted by the ship's chief petty officer. He'd cleaned up and was wearing a newly issued flight suit.

"Morning, Mister Ambassador. Sleep okay?"

"Honestly? No. She's fast, but she's a little bumpy."

"Takes some getting used to," Shelling agreed. He handed the diplomat a pair of binoculars and nodded towards the dark giant in the distance.

"That's the *Arizona*. Chopper is inbound to cross-deck you."

"Okay," McAuliffe answered. He took a long look before handing them back. "She's huge. And not as fast, I'd imagine."

"There's an aircraft waiting on the flight deck," Schelling explained. "You'll be home in a couple of hours. Right now we need to get you topside for the transfer." Schelling held out his hand. "Good luck, Mister Ambassador."

"Likewise, captain. And thank you."

"He's all yours, chief."

"Aye aye, captain."

The chief escorted McAuliffe off the bridge. They twisted their way up through the narrow gangways until they arrived at a large bulkhead door. The yellow warning sign read *Danger — Beware of Downdraught*. The chief threw the handles and McAuliffe followed him inside a large cargo bay, a wide section of its sliding roof open to the grey skies above. The noise of the helicopter was immediate and thunderous. Within less than a minute McAuliffe was dressed in a survival suit, helmet and harness, then positioned in the middle of a large, black and yellow hazard square painted on the deck, directly beneath the open roof. McAuliffe looked up. Dark clouds ran swiftly overhead and the roar of the unseen helicopter was extremely loud. The chief approached McAuliffe and leaned into his ear to make himself heard.

"The chopper will winch you straight up. It's fast but it's safe, so just relax. You'll be on the *Arizona* in a few minutes."

"Thank you," shouted McAuliffe. His voice shook slightly. He hated it when people said *relax*. Then the bay darkened as the Seahawk nosed across the sky fifty feet above McAuliffe's head. It all happened very fast after that. As McAuliffe's heart began to race the crewman next to him reached up and grabbed a winch, attaching it to a strong point somewhere around McAuliffe's upper back. Another crewman double-checked the connection. They both gave a thumbs up and everybody stepped backwards. The chief said something into a radio and raised his arm —

McAuliffe grunted as the deck fell away from him like an express elevator. He shot through the open roof and watched as the *New Jersey* disappeared below and behind him. He felt like he'd left his stomach down there too. A moment later strong hands yanked McAuliffe inside the helicopter. He glanced down, catching a final glimpse of the *New Jersey* as the Seahawk banked hard over the ocean and levelled off towards the *Arizona*.

A few minutes later McAuliffe found himself looking down at the hot, noisy deck of the huge aircraft carrier. He'd been on board a carrier once before, during a goodwill visit to Naval Base San Diego. He'd asked about the different coloured vests of the flight deck personnel and remembered that red was the colour worn by the Explosive Ordinance teams, the men and women who loaded the ammunition, bombs and missiles aboard the multitude of different aircraft that made up the combat wing of the carrier. As they approached the stern of the ship, McAuliffe saw lots of them.

The helicopter bounced and settled on the deck, the wheels instantly chocked by a gaggle of crewmen. He was met by four armed and very serious Marines who escorted him directly through a dizzying maze of gangways to the captain's quarters. A large, bald man with a fat cigar clamped between his teeth rose up from behind his desk and met McAuliffe as he entered the cabin.

"Mister Ambassador, my name is Captain Purcell. Welcome aboard the *Arizona*. How was the transfer?"

"Doubt I'll eat for a week," he grimaced.

Purcell gestured to a chair and the men sat down. "Well, I'm afraid you have one more flight to make. There's a TR-51 on the flight-deck prepped and ready to take you directly to Andrews in DC."

"Okay," McAuliffe said, then he paled. "Wait, isn't that a drone?"

"Absolutely not," Purcell corrected him. "It's a UCAS-TR: an Unmanned Combat Air System, Tactical Reconnaissance variant. It flies fast and high and is completely automated. A little like the EEV you've just flown in but larger and more comfortable. Flight crew have reconfigured it for VIP transport. That's you."

"Never thought I'd miss flying coach."

Purcell chuckled. "Don't worry, it's safe and comfortable. The view, if anything, should be pretty good."

A discreet tap on the door signalled the arrival of a white-coated steward and a tray of coffee. Purcell did the honours.

"How was London?" he asked.

McAuliffe sipped his coffee carefully. "Terrifying. Chaotic. The embassy was under heavy, relentless attack. Those motherfuckers were absolutely determined, I'll say that for them. By the time I launched from the roof they'd already breached the building. Is there any news, captain? Anything at all?"

"All contact with the embassy has been lost," Purcell told him. "Our other missions in London, Paris, Berlin – they're all gone. Europe is going dark, that's all we know right now. We're waiting for orders."

McAuliffe swirled the coffee around his mug. "I should've stayed," he said after a moment. "Maybe I could have negotiated — "

"The whole of Europe is under siege," Purcell cut in. "No word out of Baghdad yet but I hear the UN has descended into a bar brawl. Accusations, counter-accusations, threats; it's a goddam free-for-all. Meanwhile IS forces are rolling across Europe and no one is stopping them. EU forces are in complete disarray and we're at DEFCON Three. Washington is bringing the shutters down. Getting you out of there is a small victory."

"A lot of people died making sure I got away."

"That's their job. Besides, the alternative isn't worth thinking about."

As much as he struggled with it, McAuliffe knew Purcell was right. He rubbed a weary hand across his face. "How long have I got?"

Purcell glanced at one of the digital clocks on his wall. "Fifteen minutes." He got to his feet. "Time to get you prepped." He pushed a buzzer under his desk and held out his hand. McAuliffe shook it. "A car will be waiting at Andrews to take you straight to the White House." The cabin door opened to reveal four armed Marines waiting outside in the gangway. "They'll escort you to the hangar and get you rigged out."

The men shook hands. "Good luck, Mister Ambassador."

"You too, captain."

"We're sure as hell going to need it."

McAuliffe, flanked front and rear by his camouflaged escort, was escorted to a huge hangar bay below the flight deck. Squatting on one of the elevators was one of the strangest, yet most beautiful craft that McAuliffe had ever seen. The TR-51 reminded him of a scaled down B2 bomber, only sleeker and infinitely more compact. It was light grey in colour, with black US Navy signage on its fat body, and it rested on three, spindly looking legs. The wings tapered towards the single jet engine at the rear, it's exhaust vent not round but rectangular. It looked like a classic-shaped UFO, McAuliffe thought.

And that was the last thing he thought about as the crew, pilots, or whatever the hell they were, began preparing him for the flight. He couldn't see their faces, hidden behind the black visors of their flight helmets, and they had to shout above the noise of the giant hangar that was crawling with crew and stacked with aircraft. They guided him up the ladder and settled him into the craft, fixing his flight helmet and plugging him into the aircraft's systems. The seat was of the first-class commercial variety, large and comfortable, with handgrips like the EEV. *Relax,* the guys in black told him, *just enjoy the ride*. McAuliffe wanted to ask if any of them had ever been a passenger on a pilotless plane over a vast and empty ocean but decided against it. Purcell was right though, it was larger and far more comfortable than the EEV, and when the hatch was lowered and locked into position, the constant roar of the carrier disappeared, replaced by nothing more than the quiet hum of the TR-51's internal systems.

He swallowed to clear his ears, then felt a shudder as the elevator cranked upwards towards the flight deck, followed by a solid *boom* as the elevator locked into position. They descended on him then, the flight deck crews in green, white and yellow. They fussed back and forth for several minutes, then all at once they cleared the deck and stood behind the safety line, watching him, the craft. McAuliffe swallowed hard as the engine rumbled into life, building to a steady roar. Like the EEV there were no flight controls, only a small indicator board. Everything was in the green. He looked down the nose of the craft, along the deck towards the end of the runway. He watched the bow pitch as it rode the Atlantic swell, the sky above dark and oppressive. *Here we go again*.

A voice filled his helmet.

"Mister Ambassador, my name is Major Sommers of the four-three-two Operations Group, fourteenth Reconnaissance Squadron, and I'll be piloting your aircraft today. It's an open mic sir, so you can talk freely."

"Thank you, major. Did we just meet down in the hangar?"

"No sir, I'm talking to you from Creech AFB, Nevada."

"Right," McAuliffe said, and somehow that made him feel a little more secure. Nevada was a strange place militarily. A lot of bases, and a lot of them top secret. He'd never heard of Creech but he was certain that the technology being used by them to get him home was cutting edge.

"We've got a room full of people here, all specifically monitoring your flight, so please relax, Mister Ambassador. We've done this many times, both exercise and real-world. It's a hundred percent safe."

Bullshit.

"Appreciate that, Major Sommers."

"Flight will commence in sixty seconds. You'll hear the usual engine build up and then you'll catapult off the deck. The bird will take you up to approximately sixty thousand feet and once we're at cruising altitude I'll let you know. If you have any questions then, just holler. The cockpit is being monitored for your convenience and safety."

"I'm ready," was all McAuliffe could think to say as he felt the craft begin to shudder on its spindly legs. On the deck to his right, McAuliffe saw a white-vested crewman give him the thumbs-up, then swivel to avoid the —

McAuliffe grunted as he was punched back into his seat. From the corner of his eye, he saw the giant superstructure of the carrier flash by and the ocean open up before him. The bow fell away and suddenly he was airborne. The craft nosed up, increasing power as it went. McAuliffe hung on to the hand grips, feeling surprisingly exhilarated. He tried to look over his shoulder but he couldn't turn his head far enough. There was nothing but grey around him, and the aircraft bucked and shuddered as it rocketed through the clouds.

Moments later the aircraft punched through the cloud layer into a clear blue sky, continuing its climb. McAuliffe watched the indicator panel as they passed through twenty, thirty, forty thousand feet, finally levelling off at just shy of fifty-nine thousand feet. The engine sound eased off and the craft flew onwards, smoothly and seemingly effortlessly.

The view was breathtaking.

McAuliffe looked down. Below, an ocean of white cloud stretched across the horizon as the aircraft hummed through the sky. McAuliffe craned his neck and looked up at the starry atmosphere directly above him. That was space up there. Suddenly, it didn't seem that far away.

He noticed that the horizon ahead was still dark, and for the briefest of moments, McAuliffe forgot about the horrors he'd recently lived through and was simply in awe of the sheer beauty of the world outside the cockpit. Major Sommers' voice broke the spell.

"How's the ride, Mister Ambassador?"

"It's, well, I'm kinda lost for words, major."

He heard the distant pilot chuckle. "Quite a ride, I'm told. I'll have to try it myself one day."

"I can barely hear the engine."

"That's the point of the TR-51, sir. High and quiet. So, your course to Andrews has been uploaded and your transponder will tell all our outlying naval pickets that you're friendly. Basically, everything will be fully auto-mated from here on in, however, rest assured the team here at Creech will be monitoring everything to ensure a smooth, uneventful flight. Weather looks good all the way in and we should have you on the tarmac in just under two hours. Let me know if you have any questions, sir."

"Thanks, major. I'm fine for now."

"Roger that."

McAuliffe took a deep breath and let himself relax. Exhaustion tugged at the edges of his consciousness, weighed heavy on his limbs. The sun was rising behind him so he flipped up his dark visor and took a swig of water from the cool box by his seat. Two hours to DC. Two hours in which to compose his thoughts, try and make sense of what had happened. He'd spent a couple of hours on the *New Jersey* committing his recent memory to email, the sequence of events in London, the personalities involved, the faces he'd seen, where he'd seen them, who they were with. Then the attackers, numbers, physical descriptions, voices, speech, accents, weapons, anything. He'd drunk too much coffee, he knew that, but he had to get it all down, record it, ensure that by the time he sat down with the President and SecState it was clear in his head. But clarity would be hard to come by if he didn't get some rest soon.

He let his mind drift and speculated on how things had come to this.

Purcell had said that Europe was in chaos, and as an experienced diplomat McAuliffe had always sensed that the continent was on a political path to its own self-inflicted demise. For reasons known only to those EU mandarins who'd made the decision, Europe had thrown open its doors during the Syrian crisis, not only offering a safe haven for refugees fleeing the civil war, but also sending a strong signal to the rest of the world: come one, come all, regardless of circumstances. And they did, in huge numbers.

Over the years, unchecked immigration from countries outside the crumbling union skyrocketed, most of them from Muslim countries. Security checks were arbitrary, national borders no obstacle. Even after the horrific terror attacks of Paris, Nice, Brussels, Berlin and London, the door remained wide open. Domestic intelligence agencies were swamped by an ever-increasing number of terror plots, yet European leaders refused to acknowledge any correlation between the mass movement of people into their continent and the increasing violence. It was a bizarre and deeply troubling position to adopt.

In poorer suburbs across Europe, migrant communities swelled in numbers, rapidly changing the demographic. Yet bizarrely disenchantment amongst those communities was still rife, directed at western powers and their involvement in the Middle East, offering a deep well of resentment that fed the ambitions of those determined to undermine European governments, bending them to their will by using their own liberal laws and conventions against them.

The motivations of those European leaders were a mystery, and McAuliffe and other trusted friends and colleagues had privately discussed the issue. Inviting millions of poor, angry, mostly uneducated people into Europe then failing to integrate them for fear of offence was always going to create tremendous problems. And this is where it has led, McAuliffe now realised. There could also be no doubt that, hidden within those huge waves of immigration were the reconnaissance teams, the Caliphate's infiltrators and spies, the shock troops, like those who'd attacked the embassy, paving the way for...what, exactly? A military invasion of Europe? To what end? Global war? Or was this something else, something more regional, historic? Islamic armies had invaded Europe many times before but by and large, had always been defeated. Was this conflict an extension of that ideology? It was hard to know right now, but McAuliffe wouldn't be surprised if this present action remained confined to Europe's borders.

So where did that leave America, diplomatically?

The United States had been deeply involved in Middle Eastern political affairs for, well, too long, in McAuliffe's opinion. Outcomes were always hard to predict, but US involvement in the region had often proved to have a negative impact despite any good intentions, especially after Wazir had risen to power in Saudi Arabia. The Grand Mufti had rallied the people behind a rebooted vision of an Islamic State, challenging the House of Saud, and eventually overthrowing it. America had tried to prop up its long-time ally but the Saudi people had flocked to Wazir and the UN had recognised the Caliph's fledgeling administration. The payback came shortly afterwards: oil sanctions imposed against the US, its bases closed, American diplomatic missions emptied. The writing was on the wall, even back then, McAuliffe reflected. Most Europeans, and some politicians in America, had turned a blind eye.

With the political tide in Europe and the Middle East turning against America, successive administrations from both sides of the aisle became ever more populist, putting country first, favouring allies outside of Europe and the ever-growing Caliphate that was rapidly swallowing up huge swathes of territory across the Arabian Peninsula and North Africa. So, no more wars, the White House announced, unless in direct defence of the country, its citizens or its remaining global allies. Immigration and border controls were tightened, and visas rigorously enforced. America had opened its doors to the world since its inception, but her generosity of spirit and the promise of life, liberty and justice for all had been roundly abused as the world had entered the second decade of the twenty-first century. And in the wake of Europe's open borders experiment that had resulted in a spiking of terrorist attacks, America was taking no more chances.

Across the ocean, Europe's economy stagnated and the continent fell into a depression, a financial contagion that spread across the globe. In Russia and China people starved as food riots cost the lives of millions. In the US, exports slowed to a trickle. Factories closed and welfare programmes were swamped. Against a backdrop of ever-tightening budgets and bitter political infighting, worsening winters and a succession of summer droughts had placed tremendous pressure on energy infrastructure. As prices soared, the cost of running machinery, of keeping warm or making sure the AC stayed on, crippled businesses and desperate families alike. Blackouts followed brownouts in cities across America. Riots and looting erupted in Chicago, Baltimore, Oakland, Los Angeles and a dozen other major cities. Times were hard, and another Great Depression loomed. People sought the comfort of their faith and church attendances soared. They prayed hard for a miracle.

And then it came.

The delegation arrived in DC the day after several people were killed during disturbances in the Washington suburb of Colombia Heights. When the unmarked saloon arrived at the White House security gate, the duty officer verified their names and appointment details and they were escorted in. An aide led them through the West Wing and into President Mitchell's outer office where a bemused private secretary also confirmed the appointment yet failed to recall this particular meeting in the President's schedule.

The delegation was shown into the Oval Office. Four of them were military men, the other two civilians, and all of them possessed security clearances that transcended those of the man they were about to visit. President Mitchell and Chief of Staff Andy Palmer got to their feet. Introductions were made, the door closed.

Then the meeting began.

President Mitchell apologised and inquired as to the subject of their meeting. He was a busy man, he reminded his guests, and their meeting, although scheduled, was a mystery to him and his staff. If they were there to discuss an important defence matter, shouldn't his SecDef be in attendance? And a representative from the joint chiefs?

That's when the head of the delegation, an air force general by the name of Huffman, told the President exactly why they were there.

What happened next is still shrouded in mystery and conjecture. McAuliffe was privy to it only because of his life-long friendship with Mitchell's former chief of staff. Naturally, Palmer had been sworn to secrecy, but eventually he told McAuliffe during a round of golf whilst their families were vacationing together in California. The reason? Because his old college roommate had *needed* to tell someone. To share the burden. Someone he could trust with his life. And when he did, he kept it breezy, like a humorous dinner party yarn.

But while he spoke, Palmer's face had paled...

Huffman: *Mister President, we accessed the White House servers in order to create this appointment today. We apologise for the security breach but our mission is one of both necessity and national urgency. We're here for the sake of the country.*

Mitchell: *Wait a minute, you hacked the White House?*

Huffman: *Yes, sir. Our credentials are also assumed, for the same reason. Our presence in this office today, and the subject of this meeting, must remain totally and unequivocally confidential. To that effect, you've both been pre-cleared for Sensitive Compartmented Information in relation to what we're about to discuss.*

At this point, Mitchell had held up his hand. The President was getting pissed.

Mitchell: *Stop right there, General. Before you say another word, let me make myself absolutely clear, because I'm this close to calling the Secret Service in here and ordering them to detain you all. Criminal trespass for one, not to mention impersonating an —*

As the President spoke, one of the civilians produced a large envelope from her briefcase and arranged the enclosed photographs across the table between them. The President stopped talking. Then he examined the photographs one by one, his eyes shifting back and forth between the images of a heavily-damaged disc buried into the side of a New Mexico mesa, between the charred and childlike bodies arranged side by side on a tarpaulin, and back to the stone-faced delegation staring at him from the opposite sofas.

Mitchell: *Is this a joke? These can't be real.*

Huffman: *The New Mexico crash is not a myth, Mister President. The phenomenon is real and continues to this day. Their purpose here is still unknown, but that isn't the point of this meeting. It's what they brought with them. The recovered hardware has been studied for decades. With each new breakthrough, human technology took a similar leap forward. Some time ago we made another, fundamental discovery: zero-point energy.*

Mitchell: *Which is...?*

Huffman: *A discovery on a par with pre-historic man's ability to make fire. A game changer of such unimaginable proportions that it could entirely disrupt and destabilise the wealth and power structure of this country and the wider world overnight. For that reason, it must remain hidden beneath the veil of total and absolute secrecy.*

Mitchell learned that real-world testing had been taking place for some time without government oversight. Las Vegas had been running on zero-point power converters for over a month to the increasing bemusement and concern of the NV Energy board. Questions were being asked, and it was the President's job to sell the story. A new processor, capable of providing low-cost energy...

AND THAT'S WHERE PALMER'S TALE HAD ENDED. THE miracle was sold, the country's prayers answered. In the last few years over half of America's nuclear power stations had been mothballed. Energy prices had fallen dramatically, but for the purposes of a convincing and stabilising transition, bills still had to be paid, albeit they were negligible. Andy Palmer was now CEO of the newly formed Domestic Energy Commission that oversaw the phased rollout of the technology, starting with regional power providers. The lights stayed on, with no impact to the environment. Where they went from there McAuliffe didn't know. He was out of the loop now and still abided by the oath of secrecy he'd sworn to his friend, but Palmer had hinted at the plans already underway: new transport and propulsion systems, an automation revolution and advances in space travel that would push the envelope of human endeavour.

McAuliffe's recollections and his flight through the heavens had buoyed his mood. They'd given him hope until Major Sommers' voice hissed inside his helmet.

"Mister Ambassador, we're about to start our descent into Andrews. Should be on the deck in twenty minutes. Just relax and enjoy the rest of the flight, sir."

"Thank you, major."

The TR-51 dipped its nose and began its controlled glide over the eastern seaboard. McAuliffe took another look at the world outside the cockpit. The sky ahead was still dark, the coastline a distant necklace of lights. He was almost home.

And it would be all business once he hit the ground. Before anything, he needed an update on the embassy in London. He needed to know the figures, the survivors, the wounded, the dead. He prayed the number would be low, but in his heart, he knew it would be catastrophic.

The TR-51 dropped almost silently through the pre-dawn sky above the coast of Maryland, banking north towards the large cluster of lights in the distance that marked his final destination, Washington D.C.

McAuliffe yawned and rubbed his eyes. After he was done there, he'd take a room at the Hyatt-Regency, try and get some rest.

He knew sleep wouldn't come easy.

CONSOLIDATION

Days became weeks, then months.

The British troops dug in along the Scottish border, watched and waited for the Caliphate's forces to launch the expected offensive. At SCOTFOR headquarters in Edinburgh, intelligence staff pored over the data being gathered by surveillance drones, and in some cases, human assets south of the border. To much surprise and relief, IS forces held their positions, a meandering line that stretched across the country from Newcastle to Carlisle.

Behind that line, enemy troops and equipment continued to pour into the country by air, land and sea. Heathrow, Gatwick, Stansted, Luton, Southampton, Birmingham, Leeds, Manchester, Liverpool and Newcastle airports all received a steady influx of military aircraft laden with troops, supplies and equipment. Huge marshalling areas married those troops and equipment, and military logistics sent them out across the country to secure and police their designated areas of responsibility. Within one month of the invasion, every major English and Welsh city was under martial law, enforced by IS troops and armour.

British counter-attacks fizzled out, the defeated units heading north to the Scottish border. For the recently-arrived IS infantrymen, the news was a bitter disappointment.

Abandoned army bases and police stations were commandeered to house them, and the new arrivals soon found themselves guarding major transport hubs and essential infrastructure, manning vehicle checkpoints or patrolling the deserted city centres. Sports stadiums were fortified with troops and razor wire in preparation for civil disobedience and the thousands of expected prisoners. They didn't have to wait long.

For weeks the British population had watched in shock and mounting dread as their government collapsed, their armed forces scattered in defeat and the country descended into chaos. All TV channels were off the air, the only source of news the radio, the only transmissions broadcast by the invaders. Food was scarce. People began to starve, except those of the faith. For them, the Sharia had finally won out over the decadence of the west, as they knew it would. Mosques became the centre of all life for British Muslims, not only as places of worship but now regional control hubs, where IS troops were welcomed, where news from around the country was disseminated, where food parcels were prepared and distributed locally, along with essential supplies, and in some cases, weapons. Communities were to be defended in the event that the Infidels sought revenge.

And they did.

The inner-cities were the first to mobilise against the invaders, their quest not one of simple insurrection but also one of survival. Families needed food and water, and the shops had been shut and guarded for weeks. Word had spread through estates across the country. The police were gone, replaced by IS troops with guns, tanks and heli-copters. Requests for help fell on deaf ears. The hospitals were full to bursting, admissions now strictly controlled, the corpses buried in mass graves. The old and the infirm died in their tens of thousands, alone, uncared for. The dead littered the streets. For some, it was too much to bear. Supermarkets would still have tinned food, powdered milk, nappies, baby food, dried goods, something. Anything. The police were gone, there were no guards or working CCTV. It was time to act before they all starved to death.

In Leeds, the huge Asda hypermarket on the Acorn business park was the target of a thousand-strong mob that surged up the A64, torching cars and destroying property as they went. As the mob headed across the huge, empty car park, IS troops were waiting. A dozen infantrymen stood up on the roof and fired round after round of tear gas down into the throng. Stun grenades followed, their detonations rippling through the mass of bodies. Blinded and deafened, panicked rioters pushed, punched and scrambled amongst themselves, desperate to escape, scattering towards the IS troop trucks that rumbled along the access road behind them to block their escape. Troops wearing gas-masks and wielding long batons quickly dismounted and waded into the crowd, knocking scores of rioters to the ground. There was no attempt at reasonable force: arms, legs and ribs were broken, skulls crushed. Behind the front rank more IS troops advanced, cuffing the dazed and injured. As the tear gas cleared, six articulated container lorries arrived, drawing around the car park in a wide circle and rocking to a halt in a hiss of air brakes. On the fringes of the chaos, several dozen rioters broke free and ran, scattering across the business park. Automatic weapons fire chased them. Most of the escapees died with bullets in their backs.

The captured rioters were dragged to their feet and loaded into the container trucks. Their injuries were ignored, likewise their pleas for medical help. Hundreds were crammed inside each truck, and then the doors were sealed shut and chained. The trucks rumbled into life and headed towards the ring road, accompanied by the troop trucks. The rioters would never see home again.

The Acorn Business Park fell silent once more, the asphalt stained with blood and littered with over fifty bodies. The message sent was loud and clear; insurrection would not be tolerated.

Over the following weeks, similar scenes were repeated around the country, with varying degrees of violence and destruction, however, the end result was always the same. IS forces simply proved too strong for any resistance, particularly poorly-armed and disorganised civilian mobs. Those unfortunates that survived these violent encounters were transported to empty warehouses and industrial sites right across the country, all scouted and earmarked long before the invasion began. There the prisoners were stripped, fingerprinted and photographed. They were issued with orange coveralls, fed and watered. The food quashed their hunger, the armed guards, razor wire and anti-personnel mines their appetite for rebellion. Most of the prisoners were male, aged between fifteen and fifty, a demographic predicted by the Caliphate's military planners. They knew that enforced hunger would lead to desperation, the survival of the fittest. They predicted that the strong would take to the streets, led by natural leaders well versed in aggression and violence, the very people who harboured the greatest potential for insurrection and rebellion. Over the course of several weeks, the planners had been proven correct. Now that threat had been virtually wiped out.

In other parts of the country, the scenes could not have been more different. In London, Luton, Birmingham, Blackburn, Bradford, Oldham, Leicester, Manchester and scores of other towns and cities, Muslim populations welcomed IS forces like conquering heroes. In the east London borough of Tower Hamlets, tens of thousands lined the streets as IS military forces poured into the capital and tightened their grip on the city. Huge crowds thronged the pavements of Mile End Road, clapping, cheering and showering the roads with flowers and garlands. Black IS flags hung from every rooftop and window. Invading troops in Europe had witnessed similar scenes.

IS commanders were inundated with requests from young British Muslims eager to join their ranks, just one more phenomenon that had been foreseen during the Caliphate's planning phase. Queues formed outside designated reception centres, and uniforms and identity cards were issued. But no weapons. Not yet anyway.

The volunteers underwent a short period of intense training and were formed into policing units. Within a month, the IS presence on the streets increased dramatically. The extra personnel were soon in action, for there was much work to be done, particularly in some of the larger cities where many buildings had been destroyed and huge fires had raged unchecked. Major clean-up operations began in earnest. The order went out. Forced labour was needed, and lots of it.

Detention centres were emptied and captured prisoners were shuttled into towns and cities where they went to work. Guarded by IS troops and British volunteers, the prisoners began to clear the roads of rubble and debris. Countless bodies were recovered, the remains bagged and transported to recycling plants for cremation. That particular task was thankless and seemed never-ending, particularly in London. Gradually the streets were cleared and traffic, most of it military, began to move unhindered across the country.

Power was restored to hospitals around the country. The dead numbered in the hundreds of thousands, the sick and infirm three times that figure. Wards were cleared and fumigated, medical supplies shipped in, and hospital staff were ordered to report to their places of work in exchange for food rations and other privileges for both themselves and their families. Surgeries and operating theatres worked around the clock, with priority given to military personnel and British Muslims. Eventually, efforts were made to clear the backlog of those who had somehow survived, trapped in their hospital beds while society collapsed around them and the country buckled beneath the weight of the invasion. Those that hadn't survived were buried in mass graves or incinerated without record.

After several weeks of relative peace, the invasion entered a new phase. From across the Middle East and Europe, non-combat personnel began to arrive in England, men and women whose expertise lay in civil engineering, in large-scale building and construction projects, in electrical power distribution, water and waste treatment. Their ranks were swelled by others, the experts in computer systems and distributed networks, in telecoms and commercial broadcasting systems, the transportation coordinators and civil planners. Their task was to put the country back on its feet, to repair the damage, to restore energy supplies and to reboot computer networks. Indigenous employees were induced to return to work, to assist the invaders. The choice was a no-brainer for many; work for the Caliphate or watch your family die. Slowly but surely, the lights began to flicker on across the country. The same choice was given to those that worked in other industries – the gas, water and cable company workers. When the lights came back on, families rushed to their TVs. Only one channel was broadcasting, Al-Jazeera, showing footage of sweeping desert vistas, of the Great Pyramids at Giza and the ancient city of Petra, accompanied by soothing Arabic music. Over the images, a reassuring voice repeated the same message:

"Citizens of Britain, your government has failed you and has been removed. In its place, the Islamic State has recognised your plight and has taken on the duty of government. The Caliphate is now responsible for your welfare. There is no reason to panic or be afraid. Food and water will be distributed at a registration centre near you. Failure to register will result in arrest and detention. A curfew has been imposed across the country to protect life and property. Failure to comply will result in arrest and detention. Your co-operation is essential to your continued well-being and the resumption of normal life. Thank you for your patience and understanding."

In homes across the country, this cold new reality finally began to sink in. Although bewildered and frightened, hunger drove most of the population to their nearest registration centre, a commandeered council or municipal building, a local school or sports centre, and in the larger cities, football and other sports stadia. Inside, the long lines were policed by IS officials demanding identification before food parcels were handed out. Retina scans and DNA samples were taken from each individual, and the newly-processed each received a biometric IS identity card. Employment details were also recorded and detailed breakdowns of work skills and professions catalogued. After successful registration, each new citizen of the Caliphate received a large box of fresh fruit and vegetables, and a months' supply of freeze-dried, ready-to-eat meals before being sent home. Word spread quickly. Registration meant food, and food meant life.

An uneasy peace settled across the country.

On the roads, traffic remained light and mostly military. Food production and distribution networks were reinstated. Hunger became a recent, but not-easily forgotten memory. Large-scale public gatherings were banned. Pubs and restaurants remained closed, as were all places of worship, except for mosques.

With no form of electronic communication and all transport networks commandeered by the military authorities, the world shrank for most people. Now they gathered locally, congregating in libraries, social clubs and village halls. People spoke in hushed tones for fear of eavesdropping. Words were carefully chosen, all criticism of the Caliphate avoided, all talk of rebellion now gone. Whole families had disappeared for less. Trust was in short supply, and news from around the country was treated with doubt and suspicion. But the rumours persisted; the British armed forces were beaten. Burned out armour littered towns and villages. Downed aircraft lay buried in the fields of England. Surviving troops had fled the country. Major battles had never fully materialised, aside from the odd, isolated contact with scattered forces and rogue troops. It was over. No one was coming to help them.

WITH THE COUNTRY UNDER PERMANENT CURFEW, THE three hundred and forty-four thousand, nine hundred and twenty-two prisoners captured during the initial fighting or detained during the following weeks of unrest, were steadily processed. Orange one-piece suits replaced their civilian clothes. Armed forces personnel, police officers and civilians were all separated, then transported around the country to new detention centres.

Police officers found themselves languishing beneath the roof of London's Wembley Stadium, the building ringed with troops and walls of razor wire. Soldiers, sailors and RAF personnel were ferried further south, to the ports of Southampton and Portsmouth. They were held in dockside warehouses and guarded by watchful IS troops, until the last of the transports delivered the final tally.

For several days and nights, the orange-garbed prisoners milled around inside the overcrowded warehouses, debating their potential fate during the day, desperate to find a comfortable spot on the hard, concrete floor at night. At Southampton's western docks, as the sun rose on the eighth morning of their confinement, shrill whistle blasts woke the slumbering soldiers, sailors and airmen. The dazed captives stood up, stretching to relieve the stiffness. IS guards herded them out onto the quayside where they were met by a roar of whistle blasts and machinery, of running chains and screeching seagulls. Before them, the mouth of a giant container ship was cranked wide open, ready to receive them. The ship's flanks were scarred by streaks of rust and faded paintwork, but the red crescent symbols stamped on its hull and funnel were bright with fresh paint. The prisoners were cuffed with plastic ties, then shoved forward towards that huge, open mouth. In their thousands, they disappeared inside the belly of the beast.

From the bridge of the MV *Minerva*, Captain Abdul Rahman watched the long orange lines shuffling

141

aboard his vessel with mild interest. The sixty-four thousand tonne roll-on roll-off cargo ship had arrived on the coast of England a week before with a full payload of military equipment and was now returning home with six thousand British prisoners and a company of infantrymen rotating back to the Caliphate.

Home was the port of Jeddah on the Red Sea coast, and Captain Rahman was keen to get back. Three days ago, his only daughter had given birth to his first grandchild while Rahman had been tied up alongside the dock in England, and he was quietly excited about seeing the little mite. A boy, too. Allah had truly blessed him.

The *Minerva* had been placed on standby since before the invasion and Rahman had been one of the first civilian captains to dock at an English port after hostilities had begun. He'd been extremely nervous then, watching the night skies for enemy aircraft while his crew had worked feverishly to unload their armoured fighting vehicles from the cavernous hold. It had been a tense time indeed. It was different now, of course.

He'd sailed back to the Red Sea twice since then, and by all accounts, the invasion had been a success, but Caliphate ships were still being sunk on a regular basis. Rahman didn't know if the submarines were British, French, Italian, Dutch or Greek, but he did know that ships with red crescents painted on the hull weren't being attacked. Ships like his. Which meant that all Rahman had to worry about was stormy weather across the Bay of Biscay.

Rahman crossed the bridge to his chart table. The latest weather map showed an area of low pressure approaching eastwards from the Atlantic that could bring with it some unseasonable weather, but if the *Minerva* sailed on the evening tide as planned, they would miss it by a day. From that point on it should be calm and clear all the way to the Suez Canal and into the Red Sea.

Standing at the bridge window, Rahman watched the prisoners disappearing into the mouth of the *Minerva*. For a brief moment, he wondered what might happen to them once they arrived home, but his thoughts quickly turned to his tiny grandson Abdul and the joy of their first meeting, of holding the young one in his arms for the very first time. And such a name, too.

As for the prisoners in his charge, he gave them no more thought.

THE OFFSHORE BREEZES WHISTLED AND GUSTED through the huge, empty vehicle deck, competing with the guards' ceaseless, unintelligible shouting that echoed around the metal superstructure.

The prisoners were ordered to sit on the hard metal decking, cuffed hands on their heads. The buzz of speculation was like an angry swarm of bees hovering over the throng. They were headed overseas for certain. Maybe not, others whispered. Maybe a prison island off the coast, or in another part of Europe? It was universally agreed that wherever they were headed, their treatment was not going to be pleasant.

The talking ceased as the ship rumbled and began to move. Across the decks, thousands of heads turned and watched the docks slipping by outside. Many contemplated their captivity and tried to come to terms with what might lie ahead. As the ship headed out into the Solent, others watched the passing of the green, distant hills of England and wondered if they'd ever see home again.

· · ·

BUT AT LEAST THEY WERE ALIVE.

For some of Britain's prison population, the invasion heralded an unexpected end to their sentences. When the lights went out in prisons across the country, the event was initially greeted with jeers and derision. For the first half-hour, the disruption was nothing more than an inconvenience. As the hours passed, that inconvenience turned to simmering anger, then violence.

Like scores of other penal establishments across England, Woodhill prison was severely overcrowded and housed some of the worst criminals in British society. When the power failed, the violence began almost immediately. Prison staff, already under severe pressure caused by the outage, began disappearing when a fighter jet screamed over the prison and crashed into fields to the west of the facility. Three hours later, with news of a national crisis spreading fast, there was only a dozen staff left to deal with the trouble. When fires broke out in several buildings, the governor ordered the prison to be sealed, then drove off in her car. Some prisoners, trustees who were outside the main wings, were witness to at least two murders. The noise from the wings that first night was fearful: screams, shouts, roars of pain and violence, the breaking of glass, the hammering of doors. Hands were thrust through barred windows, waving pillowcases and clothing, calling for help. Four prison officers grabbed the master keys and went to their aid. They never returned.

When IS troops arrived three days later they found a scene of carnage and devastation. The young offenders' wing had been almost completely destroyed by fire, most of its occupants burned or choked to death. The Close Supervision Centre, home to the prison's most dangerous inmates, survived unscathed, with a majority of its population starving but alive. They also discovered four prison officers, hanging by their necks from a landing.

The scene at Woodhill was mirrored in almost every penal establishment across the country. Most category C and D offenders took the opportunity to disappear during the invasion. A and B absconders were rare, due to their confinement, but they gave full vent to their anger and frustration as the world beyond the walls and the barbed wire went to hell.

It took more than a month before the riots were quelled and the surviving prisoners were secured and processed. Thousands had been killed, and thousands more had escaped. Thirty thousand compliant prisoners were released and put to work in clean-up crews and other general duties, in return for food and a semblance of freedom. Dissenters were punished under Sharia law.

Which left thirty-three thousand, eight hundred and nineteen prisoners accounted for, all of whom constituted the hard-core of British criminality. These were the human traffickers, the murderers, the child killers, rapists and the criminally unhinged, comprising the very worst elements of society. There would be no work gangs for these men and women, no chance of working for food and freedom. For them, a final solution would be required.

Two Dutch cargo ships, both now surplus to IS requirements, were ordered to dock in the eastern port of Harwich. Over five days, all thirty-four thousand prisoners were shackled in chains, transported to Essex, and loaded onto both ships. The vast majority were placed in the giant holds, their shackles still in place, while others were secured inside empty stores, bunk areas and utility rooms around the vessels. When the two ships were full to capacity they were put to sea, steaming northwards. Eight miles out, on the rolling swell of the North Sea, the ships' captains ordered the vessels to heave to. The sun had already set but the IS marines that escorted the skeleton crews on both vessels made short work of launching the rigid inflatable boats at the stern of each ship. One by one, crew members abandoned their posts and hurried down to the craft that rose and fell on the dark waters. When all IS personnel were aboard, the boats headed slowly away from the huge ships. Half a mile away, both crafts slowed in the water.

The marine sergeant in charge reached inside his water-proof pack and produced a small transmitter. He extended the aerial to its full length while his thumb hovered over the glowing red button that pulsed rhythmically beneath it.

ACROSS THE WATER, FOR THOSE PRISONERS THAT believed in an afterlife, their personal vision of hell was already being played out inside the dark bellies of the ships. First, the engines had stopped, the ship creaking and groaning as it rode the swell. Then, high above their heads, hatches were removed, triggering a vehement chorus of shouts and abuse directed at their captors. Minutes later the lights in the hold flickered off, sending a wave of panic through the tightly packed and shackled ranks. Somebody screamed and charged, biting and head-butting those around him in a rage of fear and frustration. Others also began to lunge and kick, their fury causing them to lash out indiscriminately, while some stood quietly, distinctly unafraid, amused by the mounting chaos and violence that swept through both ships like a plague. Moonlight shone through the hatches above, illuminating the dark pits in which they were trapped. The panic spread, and the seething, thrashing mob bellowed, bit, howled and screamed until the crescendo of noise from both ships drifted across the dark swell of the North Sea.

"FOR THE LOVE OF ALLAH, FINISH THEM!" SHOUTED one of the ship's captains.

The sergeant depressed the trigger and across the water two white flashes lit up the sea beneath the surface. Explosive charges placed fore and aft on both ships detonated below the waterline, tearing the hull out of each vessel. For a moment, the ships continued to ride high on the water. Then they began to sink rapidly as millions of gallons of seawater rushed inside the gaping hulls. One ship disappeared quickly beneath the waves but the other rolled briefly. That's when they heard the final screams, before the rush of seawater quickly sucked the ship beneath the black waters.

The marines and the ships' crews watched in silence as the waters finally settled, leaving behind a scattering of debris on the surface and the fading echo of desperate screams that seemed to linger over the sea.

The marines fired up the RIB's outboards and turned west. No one spoke as the vessels headed back across the moonlit waters towards the distant port of Harwich.

CENTRAL LONDON
ST JAMES' PARK

The sound of the key rattling in the front door woke Chris from a dreamless sleep.

He sat up on the bed, dressed in a pair of old navy jogging bottoms and a plaid shirt, castoffs from Murray's moth-eaten wardrobe. He rubbed his tired eyes, scratched at his thick beard, then glanced at the clock on the bedside table. He squinted in the half-light; just after seven in the evening. He heard the front door close, the bolt slam home, the scrape of the heavy curtain as it was drawn across the door. It was Murray for sure, the same ritual employed every time the old man returned home. Chris swung his legs off the bed.

In the sitting room, Murray was unpacking the weekly ration box. He looked up as Chris slumped into the opposite sofa.

"Feeling any better?"

"Not really."

Chris' stomach grumbled as Murray laid out the goods on the coffee table. He'd been stuck in the flat for over two months, and in that time he'd dropped almost three stone.

He even had a six-pack now, although that wasn't a vanity choice. Food was scarce, and they'd exhausted Murray's supply of tins and dried goods a long time ago. Now they were both reliant on the old man's rations and that wasn't going to cut it in the long term. Murray was the only official occupant of his dwelling and therefore was entitled to only one ration box a week. He was kind enough to share it, but Chris was younger and needed the calories.

"Did they say when the shops would reopen?"

"Soon, apparently," Murray told him.

"Did you ask?"

"Of course."

"What does *soon* mean, exactly? They said that last week and the week before. We can't go on like this."

Murray ignored him and continued stacking the goods on the table. He was familiar with Chris' outbursts, so he ignored them and that irritated Chris too. He choked back his anger and studied the rations arranged in food groups across the table. There was a loaf, tins of fruit, crackers, powdered milk, tea bags, coffee, biscuits, some small tins of fish and Halal meat, new potatoes in cans, packet rice and a toilet roll. Hardly a luxury hamper, Chris grumbled silently.

"Looks like that's everything." Murray re-packed the rations and got to his feet. "I'll pop the kettle on, prepare dinner. What do you fancy, fish or meat?"

"Surprise me," Chris scowled.

He leaned back on the sofa and chewed his nails. Even Murray was wasting away, and there was nothing of him in the first place. The sort of bloke who had to run around in the shower just to get wet. What Chris needed was to get back to Islington. He missed home desperately, Anton too, and wondered if his husband felt the same. But fear trapped him in Murray's apartment, turned his legs to water whenever he thought of making a run for it. It was just too dangerous now, too many patrols and checkpoints, too many people willing to turn someone else in for extra rations. It was all about survival now, every man for himself.

Murray had a newly issued ID card, qualified for weekly rations. Chris had nothing. His warrant card and gun were safely hidden beneath a floorboard under the kitchen sink, and they'd rehearsed a cover story too, just in case. Murray had found Chris unconscious in the street on the day of the invasion. He'd nursed him back to health but Chris had no recollection of anything before that, no name, no address, no ID, nothing. Chris wasn't confident it would stand up under serious scrutiny.

Murray called him, and they sat in silence at the kitchen table. At least they had power now, but beneath the light of the overhead bulb, Chris' food looked even less appetising. Murray had done his best, but it was hardly Michelin star. Tinned sardines washed up on a shoreline of soggy potatoes, all of it swimming in a clear, greasy liquid. There were no vegetables, and Murray's supply of salt and pepper was getting dangerously low. Without seasoning, they might as well eat cardboard. Still, Chris wolfed his down, his hunger demanding to be fed. He soaked a cracker in the greasy excuse for a jus, then tipped the plate up and slurped what was left. He knew he'd be hungry again in a few hours, but for now, he felt reasonably content.

Murray cleared the plates away, made them both a cup of tea squeezed from a single bag, and sat down. He rolled two cigarettes, handed one to Chris, then lit both. Chris exhaled noisily. If Anton could see him now, smoking, he'd have a fit. But Anton wasn't trapped across the other side of town, his profession marking him as a target, his only form of ID stashed under the floorboards. That was the reality for Chris, and there was no way he was going to risk getting caught. Because something bad was happening to police officers.

Chris sipped his tea carefully, mixing it up with disciplined drags of his cigarette.

"So, is there any news?"

Murray nodded. "It seems our armed forces have regrouped in Scotland, using Hadrian's Wall as some sort of defensive line. I overheard that while I was queuing to get into the centre."

The Queen Elizabeth Conference Centre, opposite Westminster Abbey, had been commandeered some time ago and now served as a local distribution point. Every week, Murray queued outside with several hundred others, waiting to go inside, have his ID checked and collect his weekly rations. When Murray had first decided to register, Chris had begged him not to, not out of concern for the old man but in case they wanted to come back and inspect his flat, maybe ransack it a little, find Chris cowering in a cupboard. But Murray had insisted, otherwise, they'd both starve to death. On reflection, Chris was glad he did, although it irked him that Murray was always right.

"Scotland?"

"That's what I heard."

"What about us? Police officers, I mean."

Murray exhaled through his nostrils. "Still being transported out of the capital. No one knows where they're going but you're clearly an endangered species. Whatever happens, you cannot reveal your true profession."

Chris swallowed hard. "This is bullshit. Where's the government, the army? They can't just leave us here like this, fending for ourselves, left to the mercy of these IS animals. What are they doing in Scotland, for Christ's sake? They should be here, kicking seven bells out of that lot out there."

Murray put his cup down. "No one is coming to the rescue, Chris. Whatever's left of our air force isn't going to carpet bomb London and drive the enemy out. The SAS isn't going to abseil through the window and rescue us." He tapped a finger on the table. "This is our new reality, and we must make the best of it. *You* must try to adapt, accept the things you can't change. For both our sakes."

Chris stared across the table. "What's that supposed to mean?"

"It means – look, can I be blunt, Chris?"

"If you must."

"Okay. Well, this is going to be hard to hear but the truth is, your defeatist attitude is not helpful. In fact, it's beginning to grate on my nerves."

"Excuse me?"

"I know we're living through a very tough situation but we're better off now than we were during the first couple of weeks of the invasion. No one is shooting each other outside. There are no planes roaring overhead. We have food, shelter, light and heat. Each day is a blessing, and yet you seem to be wrapped in a permanent blanket of negativity. You sleep for most of the day, keep me awake at night with your constant pacing and messing around with the radio and TV. You grumble and moan when I ask you to keep the place tidy and your constant, self-centred whining is, quite frankly, pathetic. You seem oblivious to the fact that hundreds of thousands of people have died, possibly millions, both here and across Europe. Families have been torn apart, children lost, and yet — "

"Oh fuck off, Stewart," Chris blurted. He stubbed out

his cigarette angrily. "Who the hell d'you think you are, criticising me? I've been out there. I've been chased, shot at. I'm a wanted man." He folded his arms on the table. "I've got loved ones too, someone who will be missing me terribly. They'll be worried sick."

"Yes, your gentleman friend," Murray muttered.

"Anton is my husband. Got a problem with that?"

"Of course not, but your attitude is like that of a teenager. You're a police officer, for God's sake. Personally, I would expect someone of your rank and stature to have a little more backbone. You've been holed up in this flat for too long. You need to make a plan, go home to Islington."

Chris leaned back in his chair. "Are you asking me to leave?"

Murray shook his head. "No, but you've lost focus, Chris. You're simply *existing,* and at the same time draining our shared resources. You need to focus on something, start pulling your weight around here, otherwise I — "

Murray stopped talking. Chris' eyes narrowed.

"Or you'll what?"

"Just get a grip of yourself," Murray snapped. "You're a disgrace to the uniform. Back in my day people like you would never have climbed the ranks."

"People like me? You mean gay people?"

"For God's sake, stop playing the bloody victim. I'm talking about the qualities that once made our police force the finest in the world. Honesty, integrity, common sense, bravery, qualities you clearly lack. You couldn't hold a candle to most of your predecessors. Too worried about political correctness and offending people. Unless they're law-abiding tax-payers of course."

"You don't know what you're talking about, you silly old fart."

Murray shook his head. "I might well be a *silly old fart* as you put it, but I'm not the one cowering down here in the dark, jumping at every sound. You're a coward, Chris, pure and simple — "

Chris stood up, knocking his chair over.

"Don't you dare talk to me like that."

"What are you going to do? Arrest me? Sit down, Chris, before you make a bigger fool of yourself."

"Don't tell me what to do."

Murray pinched the end of his cigarette, laid it carefully on the ashtray between them. "I want you to leave, Chris. Not immediately of course, but as soon as we come up with a plan. This arrangement just isn't working, I think that's clear now. It's for the best."

Chris righted his chair and sat down, his guts churning with anger. And fear. It was Murray's home, and if he wanted Chris out, well, all he had to do was mention it the next time he went to the reception centre. Bullied and threatened by a much younger man. An armed policeman at that. He was sure that if push came to shove, Murray could play the victim too.

"You're right, Stewart, I'm a coward. I'm frightened of what they'll do to me. I'm a gay police officer, and we both know what happens to gays in Muslim countries. Terrible things, inhuman. It's been on my mind lately, made me depressed. I'm sorry."

Murray sighed, came around the table, laid a hand on Chris' shoulder. "I'm sorry too, Chris. I understand your concerns, and you're right, these are dangerous times. We'll work on your escape plan together, make sure you'll have a fighting chance of getting back to your friend."

Chris looked up at the old fella, his tired eyes, his thinning hair and sunken cheeks. He almost felt sorry for him.

"Husband, for Christ's sake. How many times do I have to tell you?"

He aimed low, burying his fist deep into Murray's gut. The pensioner folded to his knees, wheezing and clutching his stomach. Chris stood up, lifted his chair high over his head and broke it over the old man's back, knocking him flat. He straddled Murray's waist, grabbed a handful of thinning hair and wrenched his head towards him.

Murray cried out, the sound choked off by Chris' forearm as he tied the old man up in a headlock. He lay on top of him, squeezing with all his strength. Murray's feet kicked the floor behind him, his fingers desperately tugging at Chris' shirt sleeve, but Chris held on, pulling his elbow towards him with his other hand, crushing Murray's windpipe. The old man's breath rattled and wheezed, and then his hands dropped to his sides, his legs suddenly limp. Chris kept squeezing, in case it was a ruse, although it didn't seem likely. He kept up the pressure for a little longer, until Murray's head lolled, his eyes wide, unblinking.

Chris rolled off him, breathless, heart pounding, and slumped against the wall. He sat there for a while until his breathing had returned to normal and the adrenaline had subsided. Murray's sightless eyes stared at him, his tongue lolling from his mouth. *You've murdered someone,* the voice in Chris' head whispered, yet bizarrely he felt no remorse at all, only a quiet pride that his survival instincts had led him down a path that ordinarily he would never have contemplated. And he'd won. Okay, so Murray was a pensioner, but still.

After a while, Chris got to his feet. He cleared away the broken chair, lifted Murray's arms off the floor and dragged him out into the hallway. When it was dark enough he'd dump the body outside, in a shallow grave in one of

Murray's precious flower beds, cover him over with one of the many bags of topsoil the old man kept stacked against the wall. Nature would do the rest over time, and things would probably get messy, the smell horrendous, but by then Chris would be long gone. Murray had been right, it really was time for him to leave.

He had a week's worth of rations now, a whole week to eat reasonably well and come up with a plan. He would take his time, ensure that he left nothing behind, no evidence that he was ever here. It didn't matter anyway because the police service no longer existed, but it wouldn't hurt to be careful.

He opened the kitchen cupboard, selected a can of spicy lamb. He emptied the contents into a saucepan and set the heat on low. He helped himself to a large glass of Murray's twelve-year-old malt and sat down at the kitchen table. He lit a cigarette and watched the clouds through the window as they drifted across the afternoon sky.

For the first time since the invasion began, Chris Hunt felt pretty damn good about himself.

The MC-130 Commando transport held steady at twenty-seven thousand feet as it cruised through the frigid night air, the English/Scottish border now only six short miles off its starboard wing.

Inside the aircraft's specially modified cargo bay, twelve soldiers from the Special Air Service's Air Troop sat on web seats against the fuselage, breathing pure oxygen from the aircraft's on-board feed. They'd been breathing this way for the last hour, preparing their bodies for the High Altitude/High Opening jump they were about to undertake.

When the Jumpmaster signalled them to their feet, they switched from the on-board system to their personal Airox O2 regulators and bailout bottle assemblies. Laden down with equipment, they moved towards the rear of the aircraft as the upper and lower ramps whined and locked into place. Beyond, the black earth beckoned them as they shuffled towards the abyss. An icy wind barrelled around the cargo bay, the roar of the engines deafening.

Each jumper was indistinguishable from the next. All wore Gentex lightweight ballistic helmets and oxygen masks, tactical goggles, flight suits, high-altitude altimeters, GPS units, plus weapons and personal bergens strapped to their legs. Final checks were made, shoulders slapped, thumbs-ups given. They were ready.

The team leader, callsign Trojan One, stepped forward, watching the Jumpmaster, the transmissions from the cockpit hissing through his headset.

"Three miles out, one-fifty left."

Trojan One gave the Jumpmaster a thumbs up. He glanced over his shoulder, counted eleven hands raised, eleven thumbs.

"Two miles out, thirty seconds to mark."

Trojan One ran his hands over his kit one last time, then looked down at the landscape below. The moon was on the wane, a sliver of silver to the west, the borderlands shrouded in darkness. Somewhere down there, the target. His headset hissed again.

"Five seconds."

The Jumpmaster made a *five* gesture with his hand. Trojan One nodded, focused on the world beyond the ramp.

"Mark."

Green light flooded the cargo bay.

Trojan One stepped out into the night.

He pitched forward, rolling onto his back. The engine noise disappeared, replaced by the roar of the air as he plummeted to earth. He deployed his ram-air chute, heard it snap above his head, grunting as he decelerated sharply. He heard a ripple of chutes as his team deployed above him. He checked his position on his wrist bound GPS, corrected his flight path as he drifted silently over the border and above the Cheviot Hills. Flight time was eighteen minutes, distance to LZ, nine miles. Although unseen, he could hear the rustle of his team stacked in the air behind him as they drifted south; the small, barely visible Nite-Lites on their rear harnesses guiding each of them behind the other.

At five thousand feet, the ground took on limited definition. Trojan One checked his position, satisfied that they were exactly where they should be. The LZ was a shallow valley two miles distant, and no more than a hundred metres wide. It was surrounded by granite crags and boulder fields, an area that no military planner in their right mind would consider as a parachute landing zone. Except for those in the Special Air Service.

Trojan One yanked his elevator line and spiralled into the valley below. One by one they touched down lightly onto the thick grass and cleared the LZ as quickly as possible. A minute later and every man was accounted for, limbs intact. Trojan's Ten, Eleven and Twelve were snipers, each armed with a Heckler-Koch G28 rifle, and they moved quickly and quietly to the top of the southern bluff, easing their scoped weapons out over the terrain to the south, east and west, scanning the darkness for trouble with low-light and thermal imaging spotting scopes. Threat assessment, negative. So far, the infiltration was a success.

In the valley below, Trojan One heard the confirmation clicks in his headset. Chutes and jump gear had already been policed up and hidden amongst the rocks. His team was now rigged and equipped for combat, each man carrying his Colt C8 carbine and Sig Sauer handgun, and enough grenades and ammunition to get them out of trouble. Trojan One sent an encrypted message back to SCOTFOR in Edinburgh.

The hunt was on.

Despite the urgency of the mission, they'd planned their route as thoroughly as possible. Dispensing with their

NVGs and using the limited light of the waning moon, they headed east along the valley, keeping below the ridgeline, and striking south towards their target. They avoided the shepherds' paths and hiking trails used by enemy patrols, the remote hilltops where IS observation posts watched over the borderlands, instead snaking noiselessly through narrow valleys and rocky depressions while the snipers leap-frogged around them, reccing the ground ahead. Some-where to the north, high above them, a Global Hawk tracked their progress with its Image Intelligence Systems, feeding back valuable data to SCOTFOR which was relayed on to the insertion team. If there was serious trouble ahead, they'd know about it.

It took just under two hours to get to their RV, a densely-wooded bluff that overlooked the small town of Raithness. They fanned out silently, nestling deep amongst the trees and settling in to observe the first of their targets. Trojan One ran his eye over the objective using his tactical spotting scope. The nearest dwelling leapt into view, a grey stone smallholding at the bottom of the field. He counted four IS combat troops through the upper and lower windows of the house, plus two sentries who paced the low stone walls that bordered the field, their breath fogging on the cold night air. Both had their weapons slung, and one even had his hands in his pockets. The weather was a factor, the Hadjis unused to the colder British climes, especially this far north. With remaining British forces static and dug in across the border, they'd seen no action for at least a month, and being garrisoned in the small, windswept town had dulled their senses. Which was all good news for Trojan One and his team.

He swept the scope over the rest of the town. Raithness straddled the A68, a major route between England and

Scotland, a road that was now devoid of traffic. Up towards the border, British engineers had dug up the road for over a mile, piling the rubble in insurmountable mountains across the highway, scooping out giant trenches on either side that were flooded and staked with concrete piles. If the Caliphate forces were going to attack north, they'd have to do it over rough, boggy ground. But that was a fight for another time. Right now, Trojan One's job was to complete the current mission and bring his team home in one piece.

They watched and waited in silence for several minutes. The town was dark and quiet, its residents forcefully evacuated by the enemy some time ago. Trojan One had seen the intelligence, had heard the first-hand accounts of mass deportations, and Raithness had been no different, its houses ransacked, its population replaced by an IS mechanised infantry regiment supported by a troop of M1 Abrams tanks. All along the border, infantry and armour were beginning to build. The fight for Scotland would not be long in coming.

And where there were significant forces, so there were significant personalities, senior officers and intelligence groups, HQ staff and communications specialists. Most had arrived over the past few days and now resided in various accommodations around the town. Others would make use of the heavily guarded and blacked out Holiday Inn, situated to the south, just beyond the looted and boarded up high street. Trojan One knew this because the briefing he'd attended a few short hours ago had confirmed their presence, because a high orbiting aircraft had caught a snatch of conversation seventy-two hours previously, a personal call between two IS senior officers who were bemoaning the weather and their imminent move to *some shitty little town called Raithness*.

The dialogue had been recorded, then sent to Edinburgh for analysis. It had been processed, cleaned up, digitised until the words were crystal clear. Every vocal pause was measured, every inflexion debated by experts, until British intelligence was certain the conversation was a genuine one. The window of opportunity was open, but only just. Special forces would be needed.

Trojan One's hand signal brought the team to the ready. All eyes were on him, and he glanced at each of their heavily camouflaged faces as they gathered in the trees around him. They were highly focused, with a wealth of operational experience between them, but more than that they were brothers-in-arms. They'd already gone through hell just to survive the invasion thus far. Trojan One wasn't going to lose any of them, not now.

He gave another hand signal, and the team split into two groups, A and B. He watched Group B filter out into the field, keeping low against the rough stone wall, Trojans Eleven and Twelve providing sniper overwatch from the tree line. Trojan One watched them until they were lost in darkness, then he turned and led Group A west through the trees, where the bluff tapered down towards open ground a good half-mile from the town. Here the ground undulated, and Trojan One used every dip and shallow to help conceal their approach to the target farmhouse, now less than three hundred metres below them. At two hundred metres, Trojan Ten found an almost perfect overwatch position of the farmhouse and its grounds and set up his weapon and scopes. Trojan One left him there and moved noiselessly and undetected to within fifty metres of the main house. This was their primary target.

His five-man team spread out behind a rough stone wall. With Trojan Ten feeding him sentry positions and movement through his earpiece, Trojan One waited for the objective completion signal from Group B. They'd already neutralised the guards in the smallholding, had used its proximity to gain access to the supermarket car park where there were at least a hundred military vehicles parked beneath camouflage netting. For the last twenty minutes, his boys had moved silently amongst them, going for the tracked vehicles first, the tanks, self-propelled guns and fighting vehicles, placing prepared HMX charges at known weak points. They'd withdrawn without incident, and then Trojan One heard the signal, the clicks in his earpiece that told him Group B was back at the bluff.

Now they were good to go.

He switched focus back to his primary target, to the man he knew was currently residing in the requisitioned farmhouse. The name had been mentioned in that snippet of recorded conversation, a whispered reference to the arrival of *Turki,* better known to SCOTFOR as Brigadier Turkman bin Abdulaziz, deputy head of IS Military Intelligence in the UK. There was a file on Abdulaziz, albeit a thin one, of a man possessed of high intellect, of extreme paranoia and cold cruelty. Abdulaziz was distrustful of technology and preferred face-to-face meetings over remote conferencing, hard copies over digitally transmitted files, and most pertinent of all, accommodations far removed from the rank and file.

Abdulaziz carried everything with him when he travelled, plans and maps, communications and restricted documents. He was a security nightmare for his close protection detail, the twenty men who now guarded the long drive to the farmhouse, who patrolled the perimeter and maintained watch over the general's private quarters.

Four of them were on the move now, two hundred

metres out from the farmhouse, circling clockwise and counterclockwise in overlapping foot patrols. Trojan Ten was feeding their position to Trojan One, and the SAS man took Trojan Two out to meet them. Guided by Ten, they crawled across the field and waited. When the four men greeted each other in the darkness, Ten dropped the first with a suppressed head shot. One and Two opened up, dropping the other three. They ran low to the corpses, put safety rounds into all of them, just to be sure. Then they turned and moved quickly back to the stone wall.

Now they were on the clock.

They moved towards the house and split around the building, quietly killing another six sentries with their suppressed carbines. Inside the building, two were killed in the kitchen with knives in a bloody, almost noiseless struggle. Another two surrendered on seeing the heavily armed and camouflaged soldiers pointing guns at them as they listened to music on their phones. They would be needed. Their two comrades sleeping upstairs would never wake again.

Trojan One stood on the narrow landing outside the brigadier's bedroom and listened to him snoring loudly. The farmhouse was a family home as opposed to a working farm, and as such the accommodations were significantly improved. Thick carpet allowed for a silent approach, and Trojan One woke the brigadier by resting his still-warm carbine barrel against the man's cheek. Abdulaziz's eyes snapped open, then widened. Trojan One spoke to him in flawless Arabic.

"Let me see your hands."

The brigadier raised them. Trojan Two looped a pair of plastic ties over them and yanked them tight.

"Take him downstairs."

Trojan One went to the window. Down the long, asphalt drive, the four remaining sentries loitered at the gate in their Humvee, oblivious to what was happening up at the farmhouse. That wouldn't last long, but whatever transpired in the next few minutes, those men would be dead soon enough. They'd already failed in their duty, and the Caliphate didn't approve of failure. He watched two of his team moving through the shadows, setting their directional mines out towards the road. They'd move around the farmhouse, setting the remainder of their anti-personnel munitions in pre-arranged locations outside. He keyed his mike.

"Ten, One, Target secure. How're we looking?"

"All quiet. No movement."

He paused, listening to the quiet hiss of his earpiece. If SCOTFOR had anything for him, they'd say so. Instead, silence. Perfect. He found what he was looking for, hidden under the bed. The brigadier really was old school.

In the kitchen downstairs, the brigadier sat in his undershorts and vest, his restrained hands resting on the kitchen table. Alongside him, his subordinates' arms and legs were heavily strapped to their chairs, the contents of their pockets spread across the table before them, watched over by Trojan Two. The floor and table were bloody, the corpses of their comrades lying side by side by the back door, bled out and lifeless. Trojan Three was packing away his SSE kit.

"Forensic capture complete," he reported.

Trojan One saw the brigadier try to mask his alarm as he slapped the brown leather satchel on the table. He slipped off his bergen, stuffed the satchel inside.

"You won't make it out alive," the brigadier told him. "Leave the satchel, if you know what's good for you. I will ensure your safety when you are captured."

Trojan One ignored him, slipped his bergen back on and held the radio to the mouth of one of the sentries, a fresh-faced kid in his early twenties, whose restrained hands shook by his side. "Radio check your friends down at the gate. Go."

He depressed the switch.

"Falcon Four, Hotel Victor, you guys still awake down there?"

The tremble in his voice was obvious. The brigadier glared at his subordinate, a career-ending, life-threatening stare of pure contempt.

"Nothing to report, apart from the cold," came the reply.

"Tell him you're bringing coffee. Fifteen minutes. Do it." He thumbed the switch.

"I'm bringing coffee — "

"Traitor!" screamed Abdulaziz.

Trojan Two cracked the brigadier's head with the butt of his rifle. The room fell silent, except for the hiss of the IS radio.

"Repeat your last, Hotel Victor."

Trojan One held the radio to the man's mouth. The kid finally found his courage, shook his head.

"Everything okay up there?"

Trojan One saw his guys jog past the window, the mines in place. Time to go.

He lifted his hand and smashed the radio on the table. "We're moving," he said. He grabbed Abdulaziz under the armpit, yanked him to his feet. "You're coming with us. My people need to talk to you."

"No!" The brigadier struggled, receiving a sharp dig to the ribs in return.

"Move!"

Trojan's Two and Three bundled Abdulaziz outside. Trojan One levelled his weapon at his captives.

"Please," the kid whispered.

Trojan One picked up their ID cards, waved them in their faces. "If you follow us, Abdulaziz dies. Your names will then be communicated to your security services."

The men nodded, though the older one had a spark of defiance in his eyes. Trojan smashed his radio too and headed out the door.

"One, Ten, the Humvee just lit up."

"Roger. We're bugging out."

Trojan One frogmarched Abdulaziz around the side of the farmhouse, the brigadier yelping in pain as he was dragged across the gravel in his bare feet. Just short of the orchard that bordered the rear of the property, Trojan One called a halt. Abdulaziz stopped by the well and leaned against its curved stone wall. He lifted one of his feet, saw the blood on his sole.

"My feet will be shredded for God's sake. Get me my boots at least."

Trojan One jabbed his knife deep into the brigadier's throat. Abdulaziz threw his hands up to try and stem the blood that was suddenly rushing over his fingers. Trojan One reached down, lifted the man's feet and sent him tumbling backwards into the well. He heard the body crunch and crack as it cannoned unseen off the damp, narrow walls, then a distant splash as he plunged into the freezing water fifty feet below.

"Move."

And they did, as one, heading out through the orchard and towards the northern boundary wall.

"Humvee on its way. Thirty seconds to target house."

By the time the anti-personnel mines had killed the

driver and shredded the Humvee, all six SAS men had linked up and were moving fast across the dark landscape. As they crested another hill, the sky lit up to the east. They pushed on, and then the call came.

"One, Seven. Thumbs up."

Trojan One keyed his radio. "Received. Good job, Tommo. Push 'em hard."

Both groups were now headed north-west, out into empty, difficult country, where wheeled transport couldn't follow and tracked vehicles were no longer able. Raithness would be in turmoil right now, buzzing like an angry wasps' nest, their armour burning fiercely in the supermarket car park, the onboard ammunition cooking off and adding to the chaos and destruction. Word would spread quickly that Brigadier Abdulaziz himself had been kidnapped, and his superiors would waste time debating the merits of keeping their deputy head of intelligence alive or sacrificing him in order to ensure his silence long before he could be wrung for everything he knew. Trojan One knew it would be the latter. Every man and woman in the Caliphate's forces were as expendable as the next, but reaching that decision would require a theatre commander's approval, all of which took time. Trojan One would ensure that his team would exploit every second.

The quiet of the rugged hills enveloped them. Their route north was more direct this time, their speed unchecked by tactical considerations. The border was less than five miles distant now, and their progress being monitored by electronic eyes, their rear covered by RAF Protector UAVs that buzzed low somewhere in the sky around them. Safe beneath their protective envelope, the team reached the extraction point without incident, linking up with Trojan Seven and his boys. An encrypted signal was sent, and the drone of the Wildcats' rotor blades rose and fell as the aircraft headed towards them.

A few minutes later and Trojan One was seated inside the first helicopter, watching the hills rise and fall beneath them. He saw the border defences below, the miles and miles of trench lines and rivers of razor wire that threaded their way from coast to coast. An impressive feat of engineering perhaps, but would it be enough?

The men down there, the guys at the very front, they were all Jocks, formed into new units under old banners: the Black Watch, Kings Own, Royal Scots, the Royal Highland Fusiliers, and others. When the enemy came, they'd be the first to fight, and Trojan One knew that whichever way it went, the Islamic State would pay a high price in blood for every inch of Scottish soil. The English and the Welsh, they felt the same too, would fight just as hard. They were united because this land was home to them all.

Then the border was behind them. Trojan One looked below, at the empty roads, the lifeless, dark villages and towns that were now part of the coming front line. The mission tonight had gone well, and not one of his boys had received so much as a scratch. And in his bergen, a treasure trove of IS military intelligence. It would set the battle for Scotland back weeks, maybe months, if they were lucky. Time to prepare a little better, to strengthen their defences, to train incessantly, to accept that the days and months ahead might be their last and to make peace with that cold, hard truth. Trojan One had already done so. Death held no fear for him, never had done. He just didn't think about it.

And when it did come, well, he planned to take as many of those IS bastards with him as possible.

Keys in hand, Chris took a deep breath and closed the front door behind him. It was the first time that he'd left the apartment in almost three months, and the rush of freedom he felt was tempered by his exposure to a world that had changed immeasurably since hostilities began.

He was dressed in some of Murray's old clothes, a pair of creased trousers that rode above his ankles, a once white shirt that was now yellowed and a heavy navy overcoat. He'd let his thinning hair grow, and now it hung in straggly tufts over his collar and ears. He was unshaven and sported ten days of grey growth. His aim was to look as dishevelled as possible, to blend in with those few people he'd seen passing by on the pavement above. He guessed that no one was interested in appearances these days. He wore tartan carpet slippers on his feet because he couldn't wear his police issue boots and Murray's feet were a size seven. The slippers would have to do, and besides, they would add a nice touch to what he hoped was a convincing portrayal of a man with mental health issues.

He slapped up the basement steps and onto the pavement. He closed his eyes and took several lungfuls of air, more to steady his nerves than to experience the sensation of being outside. In fact, he'd had plenty of fresh air during the nights he'd spent burying Murray's body.

After he'd killed him, Chris had got drunk. When he'd surfaced the next morning, the events of the previous night were a blur, but seeing Murray's corpse in the hallway had brought it all back. He'd spent the rest of that day drinking watery tea and pondering his next move. After supper, when night had fallen, he'd opened the back door and went out into the garden.

It was a large, lawned area, stretching away towards Birdcage Walk and St James' Park beyond, and bordered on all sides by shrubs and bushes and a high brick wall. Chris had spent that first night sitting on a patio chair, quietly smoking tobacco in the dark. He was surprised how peaceful London had become, no wailing of emergency vehicles, no roar of buses or traffic. Street lighting was still intermittent, and the stars in the night sky sparkled overhead. Chris decided that, right then and there, this new life wasn't so bad after all.

Every so often he would get up and wander quietly around the garden, turning to watch for signs of life in the adjacent buildings. He'd never detected any, apart from the odd light in a grand old house several gardens away – too far for anyone to observe him.

Occasionally he would hear the whine of a jeep cruising along Birdcage Walk, or the chatter of soldiers on patrol as they passed the garden unseen, their language unintelligible, the rattle of their weapons and equipment a troubling reminder of recent events, yet Chris' presence remained undetected. After another day and night of surveillance, he was reasonably certain that the disposal of Murray's body would be straightforward.

And, so it went.

The old man's body, stripped naked to encourage rapid decomposition, now lay in a shallow grave behind his beloved rose bushes. It wasn't ideal, but if Chris' plan unfolded as hoped, he wouldn't be there for much longer. He had a home to go to in north London. Anton would be beside himself when he saw him next.

The wind whipped at his overcoat, and he snapped the collar up. The street was empty, and although he knew he was dangerously exposed by his lack of ID, he also felt alive, maybe for the first time in many years. He'd killed a man, yes, and on some strange level, it had liberated him. Chris had always acted in his own self-interest, but in the Met police, he was part of a much larger organism, where every email, every meeting and conversation held the potential to produce unforeseen, career-impacting circumstances. To achieve real power in any British police force one needed sloping shoulders and a Teflon uniform, honing the political fine arts of arse kissing and arse covering along the way. Now he had nothing to worry about other than himself and his day to day needs. The invasion, and the taking of Murray's life, had set him free.

Consumed by his own thoughts, Chris was unaware of his surroundings until a low-flying helicopter clattered overhead and snapped him out of his reverie. He looked around, finally seeing the damage to an area he knew so well. Chris was stunned.

Opposite St James' Park tube station, the Ministry of Justice had been reduced to a shell, it's facade still blackened by fire and pockmarked by bullet holes. The ground floor windows had been boarded up and the wind plucked blinds and curtains from missing windows on the upper floors. A group of IS soldiers loitered outside, weapons slung across their chests, thick beards beneath their low helmets.

Chris kept moving, heading towards the Queen Elizabeth Conference Centre, numbed by the scale of the damage to almost every building along the way. Rubble was piled high along the pavements and Chris had to step into the road several times. There weren't many ordinary people around, and those he did see kept their heads down as they hurried by. The clanking and rumble of heavy machinery at work drew Chris towards the junction with Victoria Street. When he got there, he stopped dead in his tracks.

Across the road, Westminster Abbey was being systematically demolished.

One of the main towers above the west door was gone, the other a jagged remnant of its former self. The roof had disappeared, along with most of the walls and buttresses at the eastern end of the abbey. Daylight flooded the interior, now piled high with mountains of rubble and being picked over by gangs of dust-covered prisoners in orange overalls. A crane and wrecking ball was busy battering the southern wall, punching its way through a thousand years of history as Londoners scurried past on the other side of the road.

Further to the east, rising above the trees beyond Parliament Square, he noticed that Big Ben was all but destroyed. Two of its clock faces had been blown out, and large spikes of torn metal jutted outwards from the gaping holes like jagged teeth. It was shocking to see, such a violent departure from everything he knew, but already Chris found himself adapting to this new world order. He'd never really been a fan of history anyway, and old buildings depressed him.

Adapt, assimilate, comply, whatever it took. It was the only way to survive.

He turned his back and wandered over to the large queue outside the conference centre. There were perhaps a hundred people outside, shuttling forward in almost near silence, the wind snatching at a muttered word or sentence here and there. Heads were lowered and no one made eye contact with the soldiers who stood either side of the doors, policing the queue, allowing small groups inside every few minutes. The people around him looked defeated, Chris observed. Cowed, beaten. He hoped he wore that same mask. He also noticed that all the women were wearing headscarves.

Comply, assimilate. Survive.

Inside the conference centre, Chris followed his group into a large hall. There must've been another couple of hundred people or so, queuing past several rows of tables manned by IS officials. Some were handing out rations, while others were processing documentation. Against the far wall stood a row of trestle tables where people had gathered, drinking tea and coffee and helping themselves to biscuits before filing back out of the hall. Up on the stage, beneath a huge, black IS flag, armed soldiers and a group of manager-types watched the crowds. A bank of bright lights shone over the middle of the hall, while the walls were almost lost in shadow. Chris felt his heart rate go up a little and he rehearsed his cover story silently, and for the thousandth time.

The line shuffled slowly forward. The room was a little stuffy, filled with low-level chatter, coughing, the cries of babies. A couple of toddlers chased each other through the legs of the crowd as piped music drifted down from wall speakers. Chris thought the whole scene was surreal.

Presently he found himself at the head of the queue. A man with a clipboard snapped his fingers and beckoned Chris towards him.

"ID," he barked, holding out his hand. He was shorter than Chris, bald and bearded, and he wore a dark blue suit that was off-the-peg and a little too large. His shirt was tieless and buttoned to the neck, and a radio earpiece curled around his collar. Chris frowned.

"I don't have any. I don't know who I am."

The official glared at him, glanced down at Chris' tartan slippers. He pointed to one side and Chris stepped out of the queue. "Explain," the official said.

"I was knocked unconscious when the trouble started. He found me lying on the pavement, outside Victoria station. Just after the bomb."

"He?"

"The man who helped me. A good Samaritan."

Chris cringed as he said the words. It wouldn't help the situation if he started reciting Christian culture. "He took me back to his apartment," he continued quickly. "Apparently, I was unconscious for almost a week. When I woke up I wasn't able to walk. I've been ill for quite some time."

"You have no identification?"

Chris shrugged. "Nothing. I asked Stewart — "

"Who?"

"Stewart Murray. The man who helped me. He said all my clothes had been shredded by the bomb. He never found my belongings. I've got no wallet, no driving licence, no phone, nothing. About a week ago Stewart left the apartment. He never said where he was going, and he hasn't been back since. I haven't eaten for nearly a week. Can you help me, please?"

Chris screwed his face, attempting to look as pitiful as

possible. The official reached for the radio on his belt and started transmitting in Arabic. Then he ordered Chris to take a seat at a table across the room.

Chris shuffled over and sat down, dropped his chin, keeping up the pretence. *So far, so good,* he told himself. He was quite pleased with his performance, and the cover story was simple enough. He knew there'd been a bomb blast outside Victoria Station, so it seemed reasonable enough to suggest that he'd been caught up in it. Memory loss was not uncommon after serious psychological trauma, and as long as he kept the rest simple he should be fine. They'd probably issue him with an ID card, some rations, and he'd go back to the flat for a couple of days. After that, he'd make his way back to Islington, back to Anton. He hoped he was still there.

He blinked into the portable lights that blazed either side of the table. A man stepped out of the shadows and sat in the opposite chair, the bald official standing next to him. The newcomer was younger, mid-thirties, his grey suit tailored, his short hair and beard neatly trimmed. He folded his arms on the table.

"My name is Bilal. My colleague tells me you have no identification at all. None."

He was well-spoken with a British accent and stared confidently across the table. Chris sat a little straighter in his chair.

"That's correct. As I explained to — "

"The bomb at Victoria, yes," the man replied, holding up his hand. "It's left you without the means to identify yourself, or the ability to recall even the most basic facts. Your name, for example. Your date of birth. Your profession."

The word seemed to hang between them. Chris felt his heart rate pick up again and forced himself to remain calm.

"It's all a blank."

"I'm sure it is."

"Look, Mister...Bilal?" The official nodded. "I just want to cooperate. I want to help because if I help you, I might find out who I am. All this uncertainty is really upsetting, you know? I might have a family out there, children, people who care about me. They'll probably be worried sick. I just want to help."

"You're not wearing a wedding ring," Bilal observed.

"I noticed that myself," Chris said, massaging his finger.

He'd wanted one, of course, had discussed it with Anton before their wedding, but Anton wouldn't even consider it, called it a *slave ring of conformity*. It had caused a rift between them. Chris had relented, as he always did.

"Maybe I have a partner, but we're not married? I don't know. I just *feel* like I am, does that make any sense? And I'm sure I've got kids. It's just a feeling, but it's very strong," he lied.

Bilal leaned back in his chair. "Tell me your story. From the beginning."

So, Chris did, making sure he was light on detail. He embellished it with his recollections of Murray's apartment, of the man himself and his burning desire to find his own family. Hence his subsequent disappearance.

"I think my name is Chris," he finished, "because when I dream, that's what people call me. It *feels* right."

Bilal nodded. "It's an interesting theory. I'm not a psychologist, however."

Chris saw movement in the shadows, heard the distinctive whirr of a laser printer, and then a man appeared out of the gloom. He handed a sheet of paper to the bald one, who glanced at it, smiled, then handed it to Bilal. The younger man studied it for almost a minute before placing it face down on the table in front of him. Chris peered into the shadows behind Bilal, glimpsed a shape, like a tripod. *Was that a camera?*

Bilal smiled, wide and white. "So, how can we help?"

Chris switched his gaze, almost smiled in relief. Almost. Instead, he cleared his throat, kept the worried frown in place.

"I don't know how this works, but do you think you could see your way to issuing me some sort of temporary ID? So I can re-join the community? I feel terribly isolated, you see, very alone. Now that I'm mobile I can leave the flat, find my friend Stewart, start looking for my kids."

Bilal leaned back in his chair and folded his arms. He stared at Chris for several moments. "Let me ask you a question, *Chris*?"

Chris nodded. "Sure. Anything I can do to help."

"Why haven't you asked for food?"

"Excuse me?"

"You've just told me that you haven't eaten for a week. There are refreshments across the room, yet you've made no attempt to help yourself. In fact, you haven't glanced at that table once. I ask what we can do for you and all you want is an ID card. No mention of food. That's odd behaviour for a starving man, no?"

Chris swallowed hard. "I'm nervous, that's all. I just want to cooperate. I was distracted."

"Nervous?"

"Yes."

"Because...?"

"Because I don't have any ID. Because I don't know

who I am. Because I don't know how you'll react. I've been stuck in a basement for months."

Bilal leaned forward. "Well, the mystery is solved, *Mister Hunt.*"

Chris felt the blood drain from his face. His heart began beating like a rabbit's. "Who?" he managed to mumble.

Bilal held up the sheet of paper in front of him. "Christopher Hunt, that is your name. Chief Inspector Hunt, to give you your official title."

Chris saw his official police headshot, his personnel file. His shoulders slumped. "No, I — "

"Facial recognition software matched you with your records," Bilal informed him, waving a hand at the camera in the shadows. "We have complete access to government and local authority databases." He saw the look on Chris' face and said, "You think you're the only person who's come up with the memory loss story? Absolutely not. Hundreds, if not thousands, have passed through the registration process with similar tales to yours, all desperate to hide their true identity."

Chris leaned over the table. "When I said I want to help, I meant it. Let me help you, Mister Bilal, please. Yes, I admit it, I was a senior officer in the Metropolitan Police, I can't deny that, but as such I can offer significant assistance."

Bilal cocked his head. "How exactly?"

"I can identify people for you. Watch the crowds, mingle amongst them, point people out, police officers in hiding, troublemakers, people like that. I can go through the database, tell you which officers have expressed negative attitudes towards Muslims and Islam. There's a lot of them, believe me."

Bilal seemed unimpressed. Chris decided to up the

ante. "I've visited many of the capital's mosques. Imams know me. They will vouch for me as a friend of Islam, for my respect for your religion and all of its teachings — "

"Enough," Bilal commanded, cutting him off. "It's a generous offer, but we already have such people, many of them your former colleagues in fact, and most of them Brothers and Sisters of the faith." He got to his feet.

Chris shot out of his chair. "Wait. I'll convert to Islam, become one of the faithful. Please."

Bilal chuckled, smoothed the sleeves of his suit. "I'm afraid that won't be possible. After all, you're a homosexual, no?"

Chris froze, his throat suddenly dry.

"You think we wouldn't know? Your institutions long ago buckled to the gay lobby, to the hysterical screeching of its political activists, forcing employees to specify their sexuality on every official form, every national survey, in an attempt to normalise your depraved behaviour. *Loud and Proud,* wasn't that a slogan your people used?"

Chris' voice stammered with fear. "There must be a mistake. The records are wrong. I don't know why it — "

"Save your breath," Bilal snapped.

Chris heard the squeak of approaching boots, saw two soldiers coming up fast behind him. His slippers were frozen to the floor. Terror paralysed him. They grabbed his arms, their fingers digging deep.

"No!" He shouted. "Wait, Mister Bilal. Please, don't do this."

But it was too late. Bilal was already halfway across the room. His bald subordinate stepped forward and slapped Chris around the face. He squealed in pain, in fear. His eyes watered, the tears running down his cheeks. He realised the room had fallen silent, that the crowd were looking at him. Some of the men, the closest ones, smiled wickedly.

Baldy snapped his fingers, and suddenly Chris was being dragged backwards, leaving his slippers behind. The ceiling flashed overhead, and he heard the doors banging against the wall as he was dragged towards the atrium.

Outside, a cold wind wrapped itself around him. He was shoved against a wall, his hands cuffed behind his back with plastic ties that bit deep into his flesh. He stared at the brickwork. A firing squad, most likely. Or maybe they would hang him like they hang gays in Iran. His gamble had failed.

Then he heard the rumble of a truck, the hiss of air brakes as it squealed to a stop behind him. Chris looked over his shoulder. A military truck, the rear open to the elements. And cuffed to the framework, twenty or so men in various states of dishevelment. Some were injured, bleeding. So, not an immediate execution then, and for a moment his spirits lifted. Someone grabbed him by the hair. He yelped in pain as he was forced into the back of the truck, his hands secured to the top rail over his head. A couple more bodies were manhandled aboard and then the truck crunched into gear.

Chris lost his footing as the vehicle lurched forward. The plastic bit deep into his flesh, the bolts on the truck bed into his feet. He cried out in pain.

"Shut the fuck up," the man next to him growled. He was a big brute with a flat nose and an open cut on his shaved head that bled down one side of his craggy face. Chris twisted away. He barely recognised his own city as the truck headed west along the Mall and past Buckingham Palace. Orange-clad work gangs were everywhere, sweeping roads, working mountains of rubble, marching along the roads in untidy ranks, all of them watched over by IS guards. There were civilians aplenty, but like everyone else, they kept their heads down. There were no shops open, and the few hotels they passed had armed guards outside them.

"Where are we going? Anyone know?" A voice shouted over the rumble of the truck's engine.

"South," someone answered.

"What's south?"

"Don't know. All prisoners go south."

"I heard they're shipping people abroad, to the Middle East," said another voice.

"Shut up," shaved head snapped. "None of you know nothing. So shut the fuck up until we *do* know."

No one challenged him, and Chris could understand why. He looked like a man of violence, someone who didn't suffer fools. Chris decided that he would befriend him on the journey to wherever they were going, make him an ally. Better to have a thug like that onside, and despite his deteriorating circumstances, Chris almost relished the distraction. It would be a challenge, of manipulation, psychology and subtle diplomacy. A test of his skills. After all, he was a survivor now.

As the truck turned west towards Victoria, Chris looked back, down the length of Birdcage Walk. There, in the distance, was Murray's apartment. He thought about the old man for a moment, his thin corpse already rotting beneath the rich soil. His murder would go unnoticed and unsolved, just another casualty in a war that had probably claimed the lives of millions. Maybe someday, someone would discover his bones and wonder how he'd got there, some archaeological TV show of the future perhaps, where a bunch of bearded twats would gather around a table and inspect old Murray's bones, speculating over the skeleton's demise. That made Chris smile.

"What are you laughing at?"

Chris turned to see the brute staring at him, and suddenly he was no longer afraid.

"Life," he answered. "You think you've got it all worked out and then *bam!* it knocks you on your arse. Who could've predicted this six months ago?"

"Think you've got it sussed, do ya? Think what's coming is going to be easy?"

Chris smiled a little wider. "Quite frankly, I don't give a flying fuck. You know why, my friend? Because I'm a survivor."

Ben Lieberman had already left the British embassy when he received the encrypted text message on his secure mobile phone.

The Foreign Minister's three-vehicle convoy had just pulled out onto HaYarkon Street when the device vibrated against his chest. He reached into his suit jacket and yanked it out, thinking it would be one of his ministerial colleagues, maybe even the Prime Minister himself, but Lieberman didn't have good news for any of them. Things were spiralling out of control fast, and if there was a diplomatic solution to be found, it wasn't presenting itself. The British, like the other European diplomats, were trapped inside their own embassy with nowhere to go. Everyone else had left Israel, except the Americans, because everyone knew what was coming.

A week ago, a mosque in Cairo was bombed, killing hundreds. Mossad was blamed, the flimsy evidence presented to the UN in Geneva. A sham, of course, a false-flag operation, but the UN was in Wazir's pocket and now IS armour was massing around Israel's borders. The populations of both Gaza and the West Bank had taken to the streets, openly bearing arms. In Baghdad, Wazir was talking peace while clearly preparing for war. Lieberman knew the diplomatic posturing was nothing more than a stalling tactic. He thumbed the keypad, read the message.

His blood ran cold.

"David, pull over."

Saul, his close protection officer, barked into his radio as David swung the dark blue Toyota Land Cruiser into the kerb. Saul opened the front passenger door, eased his assault rifle into his shoulder, his head swivelling left and right. Six weeks ago, Lieberman's diplomatic security team had been replaced by soldiers from the IDF's Unit 269, Israel's military elite. The escalation had unnerved him at the time. Now he was glad they were there.

Lieberman re-read the message, the validation code that matched the one he'd committed to memory only recently. *So, this was it. They had two hours, maybe less.*

He closed his eyes for a moment, thought about what was to come. Prayed it wouldn't go that far, but history had taught them all otherwise. He glanced through the windscreen, saw that Saul's men had fanned out around the vehicles and were watching the street, the surrounding buildings, waving off approaching cars and pedestrians.

"Take me home, David. No lights or sirens, but as quickly as possible."

"We're moving, *Sandstorm* residence," Saul relayed into his radio. *Sandstorm* was Lieberman's code name.

He watched the lead Toyota pull away from the kerb, doors slamming shut as they went. David hit the accelerator, and then they were headed east along JL Gordon to the intersection at Malkhei. Lieberman speed dialled his wife for the third time. No answer. He swore under his breath, then held on as the Toyota weaved through the traffic and turned hard right at the junction. Lieberman's villa, located in the exclusive suburb of Savyon was only sixteen kilometres away, but Tel Aviv traffic meant the journey could take forty minutes – time they didn't have.

The convoy had made good progress for a further three kilometres when the traffic ahead slowed for another busy junction. Lieberman looked ahead through the windshield. The lead Toyota was weaving left and right, trying to find a gap in the traffic, but all four lanes both ways were suddenly jammed.

"Find another route," Saul ordered into his lapel mike.

The lead Toyota blasted its horn, but the traffic wasn't complying. Then Lieberman saw something strange. People along the pavements had stopped and were looking up at the sky. Lieberman turned to his right, saw a woman on a bus beside them, banging on the doors and shouting. The doors rattled open and the passengers spilled out into the road, scattering in all directions. Then he heard it, or thought he did.

"Open the window."

"Just yours," Saul told the driver.

David powered his bulletproof window down and the sound filled the Toyota, the mournful, unnerving wail of an air raid warning siren. It filled the clear blue sky, rising and falling, echoing across the city. Tel Aviv was used to air raids, normally incoming rockets from Gaza, but Lieberman knew the truth. And then something else, something more immediate but just as deadly. Gunfire. It rattled somewhere in the distance, automatic bursts overlapping each other, the sound booming off the buildings around them.

David powered the window up.

"Move, now!" Saul yelled into his radio. He slapped

David on the arm, pointed. "The pavement. Go. Don't stop."

David hit the emergency grill lights and sirens, then yanked the wheel left, aiming for the small gap in the traffic. He crunched the front of a Mercedes, clipped the back of a Lexus and mounted the pavement, the Toyota's siren wailing and whooping, scattering already frightened pedestrians. Lieberman felt for those poor people, was briefly ashamed of his selfish behaviour, but all that mattered now were the lives of his girls. He looked behind him, saw the other Toyotas following behind, bouncing off the pavement as the convoy found the road again, rear wheels fishtailing across the tarmac. David floored the accelerator, and Lieberman watched the lead vehicle flash past their own, taking up point. Then they were a living organism once more, swerving through the afternoon traffic. The convoy powered up the onramp, joining the Ayalon Highway and heading south on Route Twenty. Lights and sirens cleared their path.

Saul held a hand to his ear, listening to a radio transmission. Then he turned in his seat. "Command is reporting multiple terrorist attacks across the country and Caliphate armour is engaging our northern and southern borders. Standing orders are to deliver you to the nearest IDF or police — "

"No." Lieberman shook his head. "We pick up my family. After that, we're heading to Nahshonim."

"To the base?"

Lieberman nodded, felt another wave of shame, and he turned to look out of the window. Saul was in his thirties, and probably had a wife somewhere, children perhaps. A mother and father, brothers, sisters. Family he couldn't get to, couldn't protect, even if he knew what was coming.

"Sir, I need to know…how bad is this going to get?"

Saul again, as if he'd read his mind. Lieberman held his gaze this time. "The very worst you can imagine. It's already begun."

Saul nodded, thumbed his radio. "All call signs, Tango-Lima-Four. Be advised, don't stop for anything. Weapons free is authorised; if you see a threat, take it out."

And that was it, cold and efficient. Saul was a professional after all.

"Thank you, Saul."

"Thank me when we get to Nahshonim."

Lieberman leaned back in his seat. History was against them, he knew that. For as long as his people had existed, others have tried to exterminate them, wherever they had resided on the planet. And when the little Austrian had come to power in nineteen thirty-three, the genocide had been systematic, industrialised and implemented with terrifying Germanic efficiency. But that was one man, one short-lived political movement, one brief and horrific interlude. What they were facing now was something else.

It was hatred on a theological level, a pathological loathing bred into newborns and nurtured by families, fostered by schools and Imams, propagated by corporate media and nation states, all of it underpinned by an ancient text that justified violence and murder to others, and in particular his people. And that violence was about to reach new, terrible levels.

Lieberman redialled his wife's number as the convoy barrelled off the motorway, careering down the off-ramp and surging through a red light, leaving the horns of disgruntled drivers in their wake. David killed the sirens as they sped through the quiet, tree-lined streets of the affluent Savyon neighbourhood until they reached the security post of the gated community where Lieberman lived. He put his hand on the driver's shoulder.

"Easy, David. We need to get in and out without creating any panic."

David slowed for the security barrier. A civilian guard stepped out of the gatehouse, his eyes hidden behind sunglasses, a rifle slung across his chest. David powered Lieberman's window down.

"Minister," the security guard greeted him.

"Is my wife at home?" He tried to keep the urgency from his voice.

"Yes, sir," the guard nodded. "I think everyone is enjoying the weather today."

"Thank you."

The convoy purred along the black tarmac roads, gliding past affluent villas surrounded by landscaped gardens. The community was home to some of Tel Aviv's most influential people, a Nobel Prize-winning physicist, a corporate media mogul, entrepreneurs, and stars of stage and screen. They were a close-knit community, friends and neighbours, but Lieberman knew he had to put those friendships aside. All that mattered now was his family.

The convoy cruised up to Lieberman's villa, an ultra-modern two-storey glass and steel residence surrounded by landscaped gardens.

"Pull into the driveway, David. Keep the engine running."

The Toyota squealed to a halt as the other two vehicles stopped on the street and waited, engines idling. Lieberman got out and marched towards his front door. Saul trailed him, weapon slung low by his side. Across the street, he saw Mrs Chernik on her knees, tending to her flower beds, the wide brim of her hat covering her face.

She looked up, saw him and waved. Lieberman forced a smile and then Saul was slamming the front door behind them.

"Mary!"

Lieberman marched through the hallway, shoes squeaking on the tiled floor, head snapping left and right.

"Mary!"

Still nothing. "Look upstairs," he ordered Saul.

Lieberman was headed towards the kitchen when he heard it, the sound of laughter, a scream of delight. He marched through the kitchen, through the lounge beyond, pulled open the heavy glass doors. He stepped out onto the sun-baked patio.

"Daddy!"

His four-year-old, Estelle, was in the middle of the pool, yellow armbands keeping her afloat as her little legs kicked furiously. Her six-year-old sister, Martha, glided through the water effortlessly.

"Look, daddy!"

Lieberman's chest filled with a mixture of emotions: love and pride. Then fear, desperation. He clapped his hands sharply.

"Out of the water, girls. Now."

His wife Mary was on a lounger by the pool, smiling behind her sunglasses, her knees drawn up, her tanned arms wrapped around them. Then she frowned, got to her feet as he strode towards her.

"What's wrong?"

"I've been calling you."

"My phone's on charge, in the kitchen."

She looked over his shoulder, and Lieberman turned, saw Saul standing by the patio door. "Get them out of the pool," he ordered.

Mary wrapped a sarong around her waist. "Ben, what's going on?"

Lieberman took her arms, held her close. Whispered in her ear. "That thing we spoke about, the unthinkable scenario. It's happening."

Mary stared at him for several moments, eyes wide, bottom lip trembling. "No," she whispered. "The girls, they — "

"We have a chance, but only one, so listen carefully and do exactly as I say. Get dressed, throw some clothes on the girls, then grab the emergency bags from the hall cupboard, just like we practised. Do it now. Saul will help you. Meet me in the lobby in three minutes."

Mary bit her lip, nodded, then ushered the towel-wrapped girls into the house. Lieberman heard them protesting as he crossed the hallway and entered his private study. The floor-to-ceiling windows looked out over the landscaped gardens, the flowered rockeries, the green valley beyond. He loved that view, was often inspired by it, and he wondered if he'd ever see its beauty again. He thought not.

Bookshelves formed one wall of the study. Lieberman reached beneath one of the lower shelves and pressed the button there. He stood up as a section of shelving swung inwards, revealing a short staircase. He headed down into a large, hidden basement as the overheads flickered on.

He quickly opened the safe, took out the family passports, legal papers, the stacks of US dollar bills and Treasury Bonds, the boxes of family jewellery, and put it all in a large holdall at his feet.

Against the far wall, there was another safe, taller, heavier. He punched the code, the door beeped, and the lock disengaged. He took out the short-barrelled M4 carbine, loaded it with a full magazine of 5.56mm ammunition and slung it over his back. The other two magazines he dropped into the holdall, plus a Glock 19 and another spare mag. He jogged back up the stairs, sealed the door and left the study. When he got to the lobby the girls were waiting for him, large black holdalls at their feet.

"Daddy, mummy says we're going on an adventure."

He saw Mary's eyes widen a little when she saw the M4. He forced a smile. "That's right, Estelle, and we have to leave right now. Are you both ready?"

"Yes!" the girls replied gleefully.

Outside the Toyota waited in the driveway with its tail-gate open. Saul and Lieberman loaded the bags into the trunk while Mary fussed over the girls' seatbelts.

"Hey, Ben!"

Lieberman turned, saw his neighbour Elliott walking across the lawn towards him. Elliott was a good guy, a forty-five-year-old internet entrepreneur who'd made a hundred million dollars with some sort of trading software. He and his wife Eva had babysat the girls on many occasions, and Lieberman considered them friends. As Lieberman crossed the lawn to meet him he saw other neighbours gathered in small knots outside their houses, watching curiously.

"Ben, what's happening?"

"I don't have time to talk, Elliot."

"Did you hear the air raid sirens?"

Lieberman nodded. "You should get to your shelter."

"The internet is down, and TV and radio are all broad-casting an emergency message." Then he saw the gun draped over Lieberman's back. "What the hell's happening, Ben? Where are you going? With Mary and the kids?"

Lieberman said nothing, couldn't even look at his friend.

Then the penny dropped.

"Oh my God," the younger man whispered.

"Get to your shelter, Elliot."

Lieberman tried to walk away. Elliot grabbed his arm, pulled him back.

"Ben, wait. Take us with you, please — "

"Let him go, right now," Saul ordered quietly, his carbine pointed at Elliot's chest. "Do it," he hissed.

Elliot dropped his hand, started backing away. Saul grabbed Lieberman's arm, pushed him towards the Toyota.

"I'm sorry," Lieberman called over his shoulder. Elliot didn't look back. He was already running.

Lieberman climbed into the vehicle, rested the carbine down by his left leg. Mary had the girls preoccupied with their iPads, but when she looked at him her face had paled. David hit the lights and sirens, all pretence now gone, and the convoy roared along the well-kept roads. They had to move quickly. The base was a twenty-minute drive away, and they now had less than half an hour to get to safety. Ahead of the lead vehicle, the security gate was already swinging open.

"Where are we going?" asked Mary.

"Somewhere safe," Lieberman told her. He reached over the girls, took his wife's hand, squeezed it.

"Nowhere is safe. Not if this is what you say it is."

"It's going to be okay, trust me."

They headed south towards Route 465. Traffic had thinned, because of the emergency announcement no doubt. Lieberman knew that Israelis didn't panic, not usually, but this was different. If they knew the whole truth, well, then things might be different.

He stared out through the bullet-proof glass at the passing scenery. Things had deteriorated quickly, far quicker than Lieberman had expected. Negotiations with

Wazir's Caliphate had soured, as every Jew knew they would. Post invasion, Europe was reshaping itself, geographically, politically. Old governments had been dissolved, replaced by pro-Islamic fiefdoms that had carved up Europe into dozens of new districts. The EU was gone, its bureaucrats used and disposed of, its halls and offices filled with an all-powerful Islamic Council of Europe.

Across the English Channel, the British still held out, albeit with a tenuous foothold in Scotland, its islands and territorial waters beyond, now bolstered by a US carrier group. Yet to all intents and purposes, the conquest of Europe, a vision held by Islamic leaders for over a thousand years, was now a stark reality. Many of Lieberman's colleagues, past and present, had predicted as much.

Since the turn of the century, European leaders had adopted a suicidal mindset, flinging open their doors to an ideology that was determined to conquer it. Now those same Europeans were reaping the whirlwind, and Lieberman held no sympathy for them. The writing had been on the wall for decades. Even a blind man could see it.

And now it was Israel's turn, but unlike the Europeans, the Jews would give their would-be conquerors a fight like no other. Even now, Israeli fighter-bombers were flying race-track patterns in heavily-defended airspace, waiting for the order. When it came, they would fly fast and low into enemy territory and deliver their nuclear payloads. And if they failed, the submarines would finish the job. It was time to strike at the heart of their ancient enemy, to pull the gloves off and finally go toe-to-toe with those who would wipe Jews off the face of the earth. Israel would decimate their holy cities and economic capitals and leave it all in a cloud of radioactive dust. It was not what Lieberman or any of his colleagues wanted, but the world had turned and it had come to this.

So maybe that was God's plan after all, he thought: Mutually Assured Destruction. He'd finally had enough, of the countless wars and killings that were carried out in His name throughout history. Maybe He thought that it was time to start again.

Lieberman shook his head. That being the case, he couldn't really blame Him.

They were waiting for a target, a worthwhile one.

Numerous cars had passed them on the two-lane black-top, but as he sat in the back seat of the dusty Mercedes, now parked in the shadows of a small glade off the highway, Ibrahim had dismissed them all. He wanted to see the faces of those he killed, up close and personal. The deaths of women and children did not satisfy him, not anymore. They were too easy, they wailed and pleaded, and Ibrahim preferred the challenge of real combat, of facing grown men with guns.

Nineteen-year-old Ibrahim had been a Hamas fighter for the last year, finally graduating to become part of the Qassam Brigades. He'd wanted to go to Europe, begged to be a part of the Great Invasion, but the elders wouldn't hear of it. The fight would be here, they'd promised him, and had urged patience. Ibrahim had choked back his frustration at the time, had complied with his leaders' wishes until finally, the word went out. Europe was conquered. Attention now turned to the real enemy, the Jew Occupiers. Finally, the Palestinians would get the war they'd dreamed of. All across the country, Qassam fighters were already in action, bringing that war to the streets of Israel's towns and cities.

"There! A convoy!"

Ibrahim got out of the car, leaned on the warm roof and lifted the binoculars to his eyes. Three dark Toyotas were turning onto the 465, the road that led to the Jew military base a few kilometres away. The Mercedes was parked half a kilometre from the junction and had been waiting for the last thirty minutes for a target worthy of Ibrahim's death. And as those minutes had ticked by, the young Hamas fighter had become increasingly frustrated.

He knew the missiles would launch soon, knew the destruction would be like nothing ever witnessed before, but Ibrahim was ready. The Hamas leadership had already fled the country. The guys around him thought that they'd abandoned their people in Gaza and the West Bank, but Ibrahim explained that pretences had to be maintained, that a mass exodus would've sent alarm bells ringing in the Jew government. No, it was better this way, he'd told them. And besides, the Palestinians were all God's people, destined for Paradise. Death was nothing but a passing moment in time.

But as the minutes ticked by, Ibrahim realised he'd miscalculated. The Qassam attacks should've brought the Jew soldiers out of their nest, but no trucks or jeeps had passed them, no tanks or armoured vehicles. The directional mines by the side of the road had yet to be detonated, the rounds in Ibrahim's AK yet to be expended on a worthy target. None had appeared, and time was short.

The convoy would suffice.

"It's police, government or something," Ibrahim told his team. "Get ready."

He led his three comrades towards the road, weaving through the thick scrub, splitting left and right as they reached the gulley by the guardrail. Ibrahim traced the wires and found the transmitter switch where he'd hidden it beneath a dead branch. He gripped it in his hand, flipped the safety off. Ibrahim prayed the enemy would be a worthy one.

The convoy was approaching fast, the vehicles fifty metres apart, lights pulsing and sirens wailing. Ibrahim peered beneath the guardrail as the Toyotas bore down on them.

And flashed past.

Ibrahim hit the switch.

The directional mines detonated almost simultaneously, a double explosion that punched a deadly cloud of metal fragments and ball bearings across the highway.

But Ibrahim's timing was off.

"CONTACT!" SHOUTED SAUL, AS EXPLOSIONS FLASHED by the side of the road. The lead Toyota bore the brunt of the blasts. It swerved right, then rolled over, flipping across the tarmac.

A storm of bullets rattled off their own vehicle. Lieberman threw his body over his daughters who were now screaming. Mary was screaming too.

"Shit!" David swore as the Toyota clipped the shattered lead vehicle. He battled with the steering wheel. Through the windshield, the scrub loomed large.

"Brace!" Saul shouted, and then the SUV was barrelling through the scrub in a cloud of dust and dirt. They hit a tree, then another, and came to a stop, shrouded in a dusty brown fog. Escaping steam hissed angrily from a fractured radiator.

"Get them into the trees, head east," Saul said, handing

Lieberman a radio. He kicked his door open and Lieberman heard the shooting. David grabbed a short-barrelled carbine from the footwell, cocked it and threw his door open too.

"Let's go!" Lieberman said to Mary. They unbuckled the girls and dragged them out of the vehicle. Lieberman grabbed Estelle, Mary, Martha. They ran through the dust and steam, and then they were clear. The ground ahead sloped upwards, a shallow rise covered in trees and scrub. Lieberman had only gone a few metres when he stopped.

"Take the kids, head that way," he pointed. He racked a round into the chamber of his M4. She shook her head, so he grabbed her hand and jammed the radio in her palm.

Mary was horrified. "Don't be stupid, Ben."

"I can't leave them."

"You can't leave *us*!"

He grabbed her arm, pulled her close. "They'll kill you and the girls if they can. I need to buy some time. Keep going east, stay in the trees. I'll catch you up."

"Ben — "

"Every second counts. Go. I'll be right behind you."

And Lieberman turned, heading back down the hill through the rapidly clearing smoke. He'd been here before, many years ago, when he'd worn his country's uniform with pride. He'd seen action then, was unafraid of death, but that had changed when his girls had arrived. Now the thought of leaving them terrified him, but he had no idea what they were up against here. Two men or ten? Or twenty? If that was the case he'd have to buy his family time to get away. After all, the attackers couldn't possibly know the Foreign Minister and his family were in those vehicles. Or could they? Either way, he had to help.

He ran past the damaged Toyota and crouched in the scrub by the road. The rattle of gunfire was louder now, a constant chatter that rang in his ears. He listened for a moment, knew the sound of an AK as well as he knew his wife's voice, counted the differing bursts. Not twenty, or ten. Five or less. Good odds.

He jammed the M4 into his shoulder. Further down on the road, the third Toyota was taking hits, Saul's guys returning fire from behind the bullet-proof vehicle. Across the road, the bomb-damaged SUV was motionless, its body-work peppered with shrapnel. He saw movement behind it, someone crouched behind the front wheel, his khaki trousers red with blood. Then he saw Saul ahead of him, moving through the trees towards the chatter of AKs.

Lieberman followed him.

Grenades detonated across the road. Lieberman flinched, hit the dirt. He crawled on his belly along the gutter, saw the guardrail curving to his left, saw the muzzle smoke of the AKs about fifty metres ahead. He counted three, four attackers maybe. He crawled further, and then he saw Saul, his white shirt bloodied. That's when he saw the body of a kid, a young Palestinian, his throat cut from ear to ear. He raised a finger to his lips.

"Go back to your family," Saul hissed. "Keep moving east."

"They're heading towards the base."

"Without someone to protect them? Smart move. What if there's another team out there?"

And Lieberman's heart froze. "You think — "

"No time to think. We neutralise this threat, move on." Saul spoke rapidly into his radio for several moments. "Help is on the way, from the base. I've sent two of my guys after your family. Stay here, stay low."

"No."

Lieberman held his gaze. "Okay, then don't get in front

of me. My guys are at your nine o'clock, behind the last SUV. Anyone else is bad news. Shoot first, don't ask questions. Got it? Good."

And Saul was gone.

Lieberman followed him, ducking and swooping through the low hanging branches. A minute later and they were crouched together behind a tree. Lieberman's chest heaved with exertion, and sweat poured off his brow. He noticed Saul was barely breathing hard.

Through the scrub, Lieberman saw movement, a glimpse of an arm, a black t-shirt, the loud chatter of AKs. Saul was on his radio, whispering to one of his guys behind the bullet-riddled SUV.

"I'm at your one o'clock, Avi, at the base of that big twisted tree. Got it? Okay, on my command give me ten seconds of sustained fire, everything you've got. Keep their heads down so I can get close. Ready? Three, two, one — "

Lieberman cringed as the trees and scrub ahead of them were shredded by a hail of bullets. The AKs fell silent as the terrorists took cover, and then Saul was moving, skirting the lead storm. A succession of shots rang out, closer, smaller calibre. Lieberman headed towards the black t-shirt, ready to shoot him. Then he heard Saul's voice.

"Clear!"

He broke through the scrub and saw Saul standing over the corpses of three young kids, their backs punctured with bullet holes. He barked into his radio.

"Avi, get over to the other vehicle, check for casualties." He turned to Lieberman. "Let's go."

The Toyota's bodywork was pockmarked with bullet hits but the engine was still serviceable and the run-flat tyres drivable. Lieberman climbed in the back and they headed to the scene of the blast. Lieberman climbed out and was relieved to see his girls in the trees by the roadside, guarded by two of Saul's men. He ran towards his family, put his arms around them, kissed them.

"You guys okay?"

"They're terrified," Mary told him. Lieberman could see his wife was too.

The rattle of tracks and the growing roar of engines announced the arrival of four Nakpadon armoured vehicles. The lead one rocked to a halt as armed soldiers deployed from the other three, sprinting left and right into the trees. Saul spoke to the commander and the next thing Lieberman knew they were being bundled into the back of one of the hot, noisy vehicles. No one said a word, they just held on tight as the Nakpadon swivelled on its tracks and surged back down the road. Lieberman smiled at his girls, stroked their matted hair, but they were traumatised. There wasn't much either he or Mary could do right now to change that, except keep them close and hold them tight.

As he sweated inside the armoured beast, Lieberman tried and failed to decipher the frantic chatter from the radio. Whatever it was, it didn't sound good. He checked his watch, its face now cracked; they were eight minutes behind schedule.

Their lives were in God's hands now.

The vehicles twisted this way and that, then roared and lurched to a halt. The rear doors clanged open. Sunlight flooded in, and Lieberman squinted as hands reached in to help them out. They were surrounded by helmets and uniforms, and a moment later they were being bundled towards a couple of idling Humvees. All around them, vehicles and troops were criss-crossing the tarmac, the sense of urgency, of imminent war, palpable. A couple of jets thundered over the base, low and fast. His girls started to cry.

"Minister Lieberman," waved a female major in combat uniform. She was holding the Humvee's rear door open. "This way, quickly!"

Lieberman hesitated, his family clinging to him, the soldiers encircling them. Through the crowd, he saw Saul and his team in a small group by the Nakpadon.

"What about my guys?"

The major shook her head. "No room, no time. We have to leave, Minister, right now." As if to reinforce her point, the sirens around the base began to wail and moan. "Now," she repeated.

Lieberman loaded the girls into the Humvee and climbed aboard. He waved at Saul as the Humvee crunched into gear and set off. Saul returned the wave, gave him a thumbs up. Lieberman turned away. He'd never felt so ashamed in all his life.

Because they were headed towards a distant hangar, and he knew that inside that hanger was a very deep shaft, that an elevator would take them down that shaft to the magnetic railway below, a transport system carved through miles of rock that would whisk Lieberman and his family to the top-secret facility beneath the Yerushalayim mountains, where an emergency government would continue the war against the invaders. Where they would survive the horror that was to come.

Lieberman held his girls close. Any moment now the tactical nuclear missiles would begin to fall, and Saul and his team would disappear in a flash of searing light, along with most of Israel's military installations, a handful of her cities, and millions of her citizens. Then the tanks and troops would come, the Caliphate's armies, pushing north, south and west into his country. Invading. Conquering.

And Israel would defend herself to the last man and woman, the last drop of blood.

If it wasn't for the two frightened little girls clinging on to him so desperately, Foreign Minister Ben Lieberman would've grabbed a gun and joined the fight.

CHRIS BRUSHED ASIDE THE TENT FLAP AND STEPPED out into the hot afternoon sun.

He squinted into the bright light, scratching at the lice buried in his thick grey beard, then set off, trudging between the endless rows of white canvas marquees that stretched in all directions across the sun-baked desert.

He kept away from the camp's main arteries, preferring instead to navigate the warren of smaller paths that criss-crossed the site. He moved quickly, stepping over guide ropes, ducking beneath awnings, keeping his head down. He needed to be invisible today.

And he needed to look where he was going. His sandal caught a tent rope and he tumbled to the dirt. He cursed, got to his feet, brushed the sand from his hands and clothes. His sandal strap had snapped and he cursed again. He ran a hand over his bald, sweating dome. The camp didn't issue footwear of any kind, and there were no shops where such things could be bought. There was a black market for goods, and ordinarily, Chris would've procured himself another pair. Sandals were a mark of seniority in the camp, a signal to others that the wearer was well connected. Someone to be respected.

Someone like Chris.

As he fiddled with the broken strap he heard the crack of a whip, a yelp of pain. Through a gap between the tents, he saw a gaggle of new arrivals being herded towards the newly erected marquees at the southern tip of the camp. That would be a long, bruising trek, Chris knew. Newcomers had nothing, literally. On arrival, they were stripped naked and given a black linen smock and trousers. No shoes, no hat or keffiyeh to shield them from the dust and the burning sun. Those things had to be earned. As Chris had earned his.

Every few days another convoy would arrive, or a transport plane would land out on the airstrip, and new prisoners would spill from the trucks and cargo holds and be driven like cattle to their new accommodations by whip-wielding guards. They had a whole team of prisoners designated for just that purpose, erecting tents out on the periphery, settling the newcomers, and all the while the canvas city mushroomed further and further out into the desert.

Its burgeoning population was a regular topic of discussion around the nightly cooking fires. Two hundred thousand was Chris' guess. He'd been to Glastonbury a few times, in another life, and the crowds there had been almost as huge, the tents spilling out across the Somerset hills in a seamless carpet of colour. How he longed to revisit that world again, relive those wild, carefree days. But he couldn't. Those days, that life, it was all gone.

He struggled to remember when he'd first set foot in this hellish place. A year ago, maybe two. Calendars and time-pieces were *haram* in the camp, and the weather never changed, so for Chris, marking the passage of time was pointless. Day by day, that's how he lived now.

He missed the seasons, the rain especially. He'd hated it at the time, of course, those endless slabs of grey cloud that settled over London during the winter months, the wind and rain, the umbrella-choked pavements, his coat dripping on Anton's beloved tropical hardwood floor. Chris wondered where Anton was now and imagined his corpse dangling from a lamppost in Hoxton, maybe right outside his favourite coffee shop, a sign around his neck denouncing his homosexuality. The thought might've upset him once, but not anymore.

He still had vivid memories of those final days in England. He remembered marching down The Mall in London, lost amongst the thousands of other prisoners as they paraded for the TV cameras, the black IS flags whipping and snapping in the wind, the cheering, jeering crowds, the speeches echoing from the balcony of Buckingham Palace. It was called Victory Palace now, or something like that. Chris had kept his head down, his face neutral, to avoid being plucked from the ranks by the ever-watchful guards. Public punishments were becoming the norm in London, and Chris had witnessed his fair share of lashings and hangings since that fateful day at the reception centre.

Shortly after that parade – a week, a month, Chris couldn't remember – he'd found himself boarding a rusty cargo ship at Portsmouth with a couple of thousand other prisoners. They'd set sail that night, and Chris knew he'd never see England again. Some wailed and moaned, some swore revenge. Others cried. Chris felt afraid, but he kept quiet about it. It wouldn't do to show weakness.

They sailed to France, and Chris was assigned to a

clean-up gang, clearing war-damaged cities of rubble. Winter turned to spring, then summer, then winter again. Time spent as a prisoner dulled his emotions, drew a veil over his memories.

He remembered the murders though.

Like the Irish boy in Marseilles, a sweet kid who'd catered for his needs, who'd threatened to tell the guards about their forbidden trysts after Chris had turned his attention to a younger, more vulnerable prisoner. He'd crushed that Irish boy's skull with a large chunk of masonry when the bulldozers were roaring close by. Months later the younger kid followed, shoved off a section of high scaffolding after Chris had finished with him.

By the time he was transported to Spain, he'd killed another three kids, all used, abused and discarded before they could open their pretty little mouths. Chris had felt no remorse: any of them would've traded Chris' rough affections for more food, better conditions, a chance for inclusion in the slave markets of Baghdad, Damascus and Cairo, where young European vassals were a commodity and commanded a high price. Where they were treated better than in Europe. Where one had a chance of living a relatively comfortable life. Chris was too old and too ugly to be considered for such an opportunity. The Irish boy had told him that, just before Chris had caved his head in.

He couldn't remember how long he'd spent in Spain. He remembered the passing of another two winters, and one blistering summer, so when they'd shackled him onto the truck and transported him to the airport, Chris was glad to be leaving.

He remembered the flight, chained to metal decking with two hundred other prisoners on a cargo plane that had taken off from Malaga airport and headed south-east for several hours. That wasn't good, Chris remembered thinking. The Caliphate was the last place any of them wanted to be.

He remembered being herded down the ramp and into the blast of the plane's turboprop engines, the sting of sand and dust in his eyes and mouth, the agonising lash of a whip on his back and legs, the feeling of panic when the plane taxied and took off again, leaving them stranded. He remembered seeing the ocean of white tents for the first time, the brutality of the guards, the terrible pain of his sunburnt skin, the hunger and dehydration of those first few weeks. Of those original two hundred prisoners, Chris was one of only a dozen survivors, and he was proud of that. Because here, in this city of slaves, survival was everything.

The purpose of such a city soon revealed itself. They were building a new capital, out beyond the low hills to the east. A limited nuclear exchange had destroyed a dozen cities in Israel and across the Caliphate, and a huge rebuilding programme had been implemented. What Wazir envisioned was not a modern metropolis teeming with towering skyscrapers of glass and steel. No, it was to be something else, a reconstruction of past empires and civilisations, a city built of stone, granite and marble, with magnificent palaces and vast public squares, with residential complexes and hotels inspired by the hanging gardens of Babylon, with sumptuous villas for the elite, clustered around a vast network of man-made canals. Where every road was like a spoke on a wheel, all leading to a magnificent central hub, the largest mosque the world had ever seen. The city was to be a modern wonder of the world, its hidden infrastructure humming with cutting-edge technology. The glorious capital of the New Caliphate.

And Chris had no intention of ever working there.

Because they'd discovered something else out there, buried deep beneath the shifting sands, something of huge religious significance. A decree had been handed down, declarations made. The city was to be built by the hand of man alone. And that meant slave labour, to carve the stone from distant quarries and mines, to transport it to the capital and heave it into position, to hack into the earth and excavate the huge network of canals. Which explained the endless stream of prisoners ferried in from Europe and elsewhere.

Hundreds died every month, and by a variety of means: heatstroke, accidents, exhaustion, illness, punishment, escape, murder, all providing the workers' cemetery with a steady stream of business. Which was good news for Chris, because transporting the dead was his profession.

The hot sun was beginning to dip towards the horizon as he reached the perimeter of the camp. He paused to catch his breath, took a swig of water from the flask on his worn leather belt. He looked out over the barren landscape, a sea of emptiness as far as the eye could see. There were no fences or guard towers around the camp. People escaped of course, and no one ever stopped them, not even the guards, because only death awaited them out there, in every direction beyond the sun-baked horizon. It's why Chris had never tried. He wasn't stupid, or suicidal. But he did want to leave.

He turned to the west. Half a mile away was the prisoner burial ground, and Chris could see the multitude of small, white grave markers shimmering in the late afternoon heat. He set off across the desert floor, limping on his broken sandal.

By the time he reached the cemetery, the shadows were beginning to lengthen. There were a handful of other prisoners dotted around, wandering past the rough, white-washed planks that served as headstones, pausing here and there, maybe visiting the graves of friends or family. The cemetery was a place of peace, some said, of pause and reflection. Chris didn't give a shit about any of that. For him, it was a treasure trove, a gateway to another life.

A way out.

He moved slowly towards the graves at the very edge of the cemetery, where the original incumbents, the prisoners who were first to arrive and die here, were buried. No one remembered them anymore, the smooth sand surrounding the staggered rows of bleached and peeling headboards untouched by the feet of others. Chris stopped and turned around. The nearest people were a couple of hundred metres away, while others were heading back to camp, tiny stick figures in the distance. He was alone.

He dropped to his knees, sweeping away sand from the base of the timber marker, using an old metal spoon to dig beneath the ground. He'd stop every few minutes and look around, his head swivelling left and right like a nervous meerkat. The sun had almost set now, the sky a deep blue, the heat slowly dissipating.

He burrowed like a mole until his fingers found metal and pulled the battered biscuit tin out of its hole. He prised it open, unfolded the bulging plastic bag inside, and carefully poured several gold teeth into the palm of his hand. He fingered them, satisfied the weight and quality would provide sufficient financial incentive. He sealed the bag with an elastic band, then he retrieved a cake of soap, scissors and a razor from the tin, and squeezed them into the pouch on his belt.

The teeth were his lifeline, his ticket out of there, smashed from the mouths of the dead by Chris as he transported corpses from the camp to the graveyard in his mule cart. The first one had been grisly enough, folding back the shroud, fingering the mouth for treasure, breaking the jaw with a club hammer and using pliers to wrench the tooth from the gum. But now he didn't think about it, and it had surprised him how many people had gold fillings. And gold bought many things, black market goods, loyalty, silence – and soon, a ride back to Europe.

His name was Hamid, a gruff old sergeant in the Transport Corps, a man responsible for the trucks and Humvees used by the guards, for the droves of donkeys that worked the camp and the distant construction site. Every day Chris would drive his animal back to the sprawling pens, unhitch his cart and hand it all back to Hamid. In return, Hamid would engage Chris in conversations of broken English. As time passed, a friendship had formed, and Chris' Arabic was now pretty good. He'd learned something else too, something very useful: Corporal Hamid was a bitter man.

His only son had died during the battle for Scotland, and Hamid was informed of his child's death by his line officer, then ordered back to his donkeys. No details or context, just a cold declaration in a hot, humid office. Hamid had lost his wife a few years ago, and now he had nothing. Hamid mourned his son's loss, made even more painful by the lack of a grave or the opportunity to pray for his soul at the scene of his death. And respect had to be paid, Hamid was adamant about that.

Chris, the seasoned survivalist, had sensed the opportunity.

He knew Scotland, had visited there many times. If Hamid was unable to leave, maybe Chris could go in his place, recite the prayers for his son? If only Hamid could help him? After all, with thousands transiting the camp on a weekly basis, who would miss him? He could simply disappear.

Hamid had been reluctant to talk at first, but Chris had drawn him out, stoked the man's simmering bitterness. There was a way, Hamid had finally told him. A plane landed once a fortnight, a smaller aircraft that brought supplies in from Eilat.

They were in Egypt? Chris had asked.

That was classified information, Hamid had warned him.

Chris had persisted.

The Arabian desert, Hamid had whispered.

Saudi Arabia, Chris realised.

It wasn't huge news. Prisoners had guessed as much anyway, but knowing for certain changed things. Being held so deep in the Caliphate, there was next to no chance of escaping. Unless Hamid could be manipulated.

And so Chris had worked him, and now he knew about the plane, the friendly loader who came from the same town as Hamid, who would turn a blind eye to someone sneaking aboard the aircraft and hiding amongst the empty crates and cargo nets, someone who might smuggle him out of the airport at Eilat, feed and clothe him, and point him in the direction of the Mediterranean ports.

But all of that would cost money, Hamid had told him, and Chris had nothing. It was pointless to even speculate.

That's when Chris had taken a deep breath and mentioned the bag that probably weighed several ounces, the gold teeth that could be melted down and used as payment. Hamid had expressed admiration for Chris' methods. He also wanted in on the deal. Chris had agreed.

A plan was formed, messages passed back and forth

between Chris, Hamid and Eilat. Finally, the green light was given, and the pieces were now in play.

The sun had set, the sky to the west painted a deep red, already darkening overhead as night fell rapidly. Chris made a small hole in the bag of teeth, looped a length of string through it, then hung the bag around his neck.

His heart beat fast at the thought of the plane, now en route to the airstrip. Soon it would land, unload and take off a couple of hours after sunset. Chris knew he had to move fast, had to negotiate the fringes of the camp and head north, to the road beyond the camp's northern boundary.

On the other side of that road, behind a razor wire fence, was the sprawling, floodlit army barracks, home for the guards that policed them. Soon, Hamid would drive his truck out of that barracks and onto the road. He would head eastwards for half a kilometre then, at the turn-off to the airstrip, he would slow down long enough for Chris to dart from the roadside ditch and climb in the back. Then Hamid would drive north, out to the airstrip, where he'd wait for the plane to land. When it did he would offer the crew coffee and sweetbreads. That would be the signal, Chris' chance to slip out of the truck and into the plane's hold while Hamid and his loader friend distracted the pilots. All Chris had to do was hide and wait.

Then he would be free.

He stood up, looked around. The cemetery was blanketed in darkness now, and daylight was nothing more than a thin crimson strip on the far horizon. Above his head, stars littered the heavens and the temperature had cooled considerably. It was time. Chris set off, his passport to freedom hanging from a string around his neck.

He moved quickly towards the camp across the hard-packed dirt, guided by the distant cooking fires springing up in the darkness.

He was headed towards an unfamiliar district of the camp. Respected sandal-wearer or not, Chris knew that in a makeshift city of two hundred thousand hopeless and desperate men, anything could happen, especially at night. It wasn't unusual to hear the screams of the dying drifting across the tented metropolis after sunset, the victims of feuds, robberies or territorial disputes. Sometimes it was nothing more than a wrong look, the wrong skin colour. Chris rarely left his tent at night, and those that did knew the risks. Tonight, Chris had no choice.

The outlying tents loomed ahead. He plunged into the maze of alleyways beyond, guided by the sky to the north that was bright with the artificial glow of the barrack flood-lights. He was in unknown territory now, the paths between the tightly packed tents dark and narrow.

He snuck past the clearings, the communal spaces where cooking fires burned and people gathered to eat and talk. The men in this part of the camp were mostly from the horn of Africa, the old countries of Sudan, Eritrea and Somalia, a region with a long history of providing slave labour to their Arabian masters across the Red Sea. They were a lively bunch, Chris knew, but volatile and unpredictable. Best to avoid.

He heard laughter ahead and slowed. Through a gap between the tents, he saw a large group of black men gathered around a fire, jabbering in their quick-fire tongue. Chris swore quietly, knowing he would have to adjust his course to avoid them, costing valuable time. He doubled back and picked up the pace, weaving through the tightly packed tents, ducking beneath guide ropes, hugging the shadows. Above him, the lights from the barracks were getting brighter. The pre-arranged pickup point was further to the east, the unlit junction where Chris would wait in a shallow ditch. Hamid's truck had a broken headlight, and when he saw it he would —

His foot caught on something and he pitched forward, falling headlong into a web of tent ropes. He quickly untangled himself and scrambled to his feet. A boy was squatting behind a tent, trousers around his ankles, shitting on the sand. He shouted angrily at Chris.

"Dirty little cunt!" Chris snapped back.

The boy was a Somali, a skinny teenager with a shaved head. He used a handful of sand to clean his backside and stood, hitching his trousers around his waist. Chris gave the boy a filthy look and walked away. The boy shouted after him, his voice louder with each word. Chris swore, doubled back.

"Shhh!" he hissed, putting his finger to his lips. The boy continued ranting, and Chris closed the gap between them, held his hands up in surrender, patted the boy on the shoulder. "I'm sorry, okay? You okay? All good?"

The boy pointed at him and laughed, white teeth gleaming in the shadows.

"Yes, ha, ha, very fucking funny," Chris said, smiling too.

Then the boy stopped smiling. He cocked his chin, said something, a question maybe. Maybe something like, *you're trespassing.*

Chris was eager to be gone. "Sorry," he smiled, clasping his hands together. Then he turned and walked away. The boy started shouting again, louder this time. Any second now someone would hear, investigate.

Chris turned back, punched the kid in the face as hard as he could. The boy fell against the side of the tent and

Chris fell on top of him, his hands gripping his skinny little neck, his thumbs digging into his soft windpipe. The kid's eyes bulged, and Chris had that feeling again, the one of immense power he'd experienced with the other boys. He leaned over him, transferring his body weight onto his hands, pressing his thumbs down deeper, harder. He had to make this quick.

The blow to his ribs knocked the wind from his lungs. He looked down, saw the boy's hand gripped around a knife handle, felt the cold blade inside him. He stifled a scream and rolled away, the knife slipping out of his body. The boy coughed and choked, lunged weakly. Chris scrambled to his feet and kicked the boy in the stomach as hard as he could. The kid curled up on the sand and Chris stamped on his wrist until the boy released the knife. He scooped it up, a crude, ugly weapon with a rough-hewn handle and a blade about four inches long. Chis dropped to his knees and plunged it into the boy, again and again, stabbing his mouth, his throat, neck, chest, anywhere that might stop him from making any more noise. He'd stabbed him several more times before Chris realised the kid wasn't trying to defend himself any longer. Blood flowed from dozens of wounds, and the boy stared at Chris with watery eyes, his lips moving weakly, his throat gurgling. Chris scooped a handful of sand and jammed it in the kid's mouth. He clambered to his feet and staggered away, throwing the knife into the darkness.

He had to put distance between him and the boy now. He kept moving, ducking, lifting his feet over the ropes, willing himself forward. Behind him, in the darkness, he heard shouts and screams. He weaved between dozens of tents, watching the sky overhead as it brightened. He stumbled over another cluster of guide ropes and suddenly the ground opened up before him.

He'd made it.

Ahead of him, across two hundred metres of sand and scrub, lay the road. Beyond that, the army barracks, bathed in bright light. It was quiet, as it always was. Chris limped out into the darkness, walking eastwards, parallel to the road. Soon the camp was behind him, and the peace and darkness of the desert enveloped him.

He was breathing hard now, the wound in his left side throbbing incessantly. He pressed a hand to his ribs, felt the wetness of his blood. Hamid would help. The truck would have a first aid kit, something he could use to dress the wound, at least until he got medical help in Eilat. Chris' Arabic was good enough, his skin burned brown by the desert sun, his beard and bald head signalling to others that he was a man of faith. He had every confidence that he would pass muster.

He staggered and fell, crying out as the pain shot through his chest. He pushed himself to his knees, felt his tunic sticking to his side, his trousers wet with blood. For the first time, Chris began to panic. His heart beat faster, transporting the pain around his body. He got to his feet, heading for a point somewhere out there in the darkness. His breath was short, his chest heaving in ragged gasps, his eyes blurring in pain.

And then he was there.

The signpost rose above him, the aircraft symbol black against the white background. Chris fell into the ditch and rolled onto his back, gasping for breath. He reached for his side, now covered with bloodied sand and grit. He looked up at the stars overhead, a magical carpet that covered the sky. It was beautiful, Chris realised. He'd never really paid much attention before but right now it seemed important.

His eyelids felt heavy and he closed them.

No!

They snapped open. Then he heard it.

The truck.

He rolled over onto his belly and crawled up the short incline to the edge of the road. The truck was headed his way, its single headlight blinding him, forcing him to blink and turn away. Hamid would help him, yes he would. For the gold around his neck. Chris reached for it, squeezed the bag with a bloodied hand, reassured. The truck loomed large, the engine rumbling, the light blinding. Chris forced himself to stand as the truck slowed by the ditch, the vehicle turning left in a lazy arc. Chris staggered onto the road, his bare feet slapping on the tarmac. He'd lost his sandals, he realised, but it didn't matter. The truck was just ahead and he staggered after it, reaching for the tailgate, his fingers brushing metal —

And slipped off, his legs giving way beneath him. He fell face first onto the road and lay there, panting. The rumble of the truck faded, then it was gone. Chris tried to get up, managed to get to his knees, and then his head swam and he rolled onto his back.

He tasted the metallic tang of blood in his mouth and coughed. He found it hard to breathe, to inflate his lungs, as if a weight were pressing down on him. *I'll rest,* Chris decided, just for short while. Then he'd chase down Hamid's slow-moving truck, climb inside. Get the plan back on track. Escape.

Overhead the stars glittered.

He felt a rushing in his ears, and Chris panicked. He tried to take a breath, to scream and curse at the world, because he knew what was coming, the realisation, the finality, worse than the pain that consumed him.

That Chris Hunt was no longer a survivor.

That his life was about to end in a stinking death camp far from all he knew and loved. That his body would be found, the bag snapped from his neck, his corpse transported to the graveyard where he'd be planted in the dirt, covered with sand, then quickly forgotten.

The pain spiked, then eased. The stars dimmed and vanished.

Chris Hunt closed his eyes and died.

HAVE YOUR SAY

Did you enjoy ***The Lost Chapters***?

I hope you did.

If you could spare a moment to rate ***The Lost Chapters*** on Amazon, or leave a review, I would be much obliged.

Many thanks for your time.

Printed in Great Britain
by Amazon

54567268R00139